"I hope you're not one of those black-widow serial killers."

"You found me out," Lila said. "Now I'm going to kiss you to death."

"You sound awfully chipper when you talk about murder," Clint said, well aware that he'd stopped trying to get her to open up to him.

Avoiding the gearshift, she pressed against him, parting her lips and welcoming his tongue. The sweet taste of her mouth lured him closer, deeper.

Finally she pulled back. "Thanks," she said, looking him in the eyes, "for offering to listen. I need this more."

Absorbing the meaning behind her words, he nodded slowly.

He was her distraction. Not that he felt *used*. For whatever reason she felt safe with him, confident that he understood this was just a fling. That it would all come to an end the day the movie wrapped up and she left.

She'd said she needed this, and he was happy to give it to her. Hell, he'd give her anything she wanted for as long as she'd let him.

He cupped her chin and brought her face closer. "Kiss me."

Dear Reader,

A few months ago, the town of Blackfoot Falls got shaken up by a movie being shot in the area—a story you can read in my previous book, *Wild for You*. In *Hot Winter Nights*, the movie crew has moved camp to a mile outside of town. Local cowboys have caught the acting bug and are lining up to be hired as extras in the Western indie film. Not so for Clint Landers, the younger brother of Nathan Landers from *Behind Closed Doors*. Clint wants no part of the Hollywood scene, and no one can convince him otherwise. That is, until he delivers a trailer of horses to the set and meets hair and makeup artist Lila Loveridge. Before too long poor Clint is gritting his teeth and agreeing to a lot more than he bargained for, all in the hope that lovely Lila will be waiting for him at the other end of the Big Sky Country rainbow. What he doesn't know is that Lila is more than willing to share some special effects with the hotter-than-hot cowboy.

A couple years back, one of the reality shows that had to do with makeovers came to shoot an episode in the small town where I live. The cast and their huge painted bus were here for at least a day, maybe two. I don't know for sure because I stayed in hiding for a week...just to be on the safe side. Yeah, cameras and I don't get along. And now they're in most cell phones and tablets. I'm trying not to take it personally.

Happy reading!

Debbi Rawlins

Debbi Rawlins

Hot Winter Nights

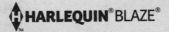

HARLEQUIN® BLAZE®

Recycling programs
for this product may
not exist in your area.

ISBN-13: 978-0-373-79921-3

Hot Winter Nights

Printed in U.S.A.

Debbi Rawlins grew up in the country and loves Western movies and books. Her first crush was on a cowboy—okay, he was an actor in the role of a cowboy, but she was only eleven, so it counts. It was Houston, Texas, where she first started writing for Harlequin, and now she has her own ranch...of sorts. Instead of horses, she has four dogs, four cats, a trio of goats and free-range cattle on a few acres in gorgeous rural Utah.

To get the inside scoop on Harlequin Blaze and its talented writers, visit Facebook.com/BlazeAuthors.

All backlist available in ebook format.

Visit the Author Profile page at Harlequin.com for more titles.

1

"YOU'RE SUPPOSED TO be dead." Staring over the woman's shoulder, Lila Loveridge stopped in the middle of touching up Penelope's dark roots.

"Don't sound so disappointed." Penelope picked up the script, with the revisions marked in a brilliant pink, and held it against her chest. "You're not supposed to see that, anyway."

Oh, for goodness' sake, she'd left it in plain sight on her lap. It was obvious she wanted her to see. "When did Jason make those changes?"

"I shouldn't be discussing this with you," Penelope said with her usual air of superiority, which was one of the many reasons the film crew didn't like her.

An icy gust shook the small trailer, and Lila shivered. The cold December wind that had been sweeping down from the Rockies for three days straight had everyone grumbling. They should've been wrapping up and getting out of Montana by now. Not camped a mile outside the small town of Blackfoot Falls, the ragtag trailers where they worked and slept powered by generators that could barely keep up with the frigid overnight temperatures.

On top of all that, they were three weeks behind schedule.

Of course delays were to be expected in the movie business. But that hadn't stopped morale from plummeting more and more each day as they got closer to Christmas. All the changes to both script and routine brought on by their new investor sure hadn't helped.

Penelope cleared her throat.

Lila glanced at her. "Did you say something?"

"I said, since you already saw the pink pages, I might as well tell you. The director thought I interpreted the role of Dominique so masterfully he said it would be a crime for my character not to be in the sequel."

Translation—Jason was still sleeping with her.

It wasn't news. Everyone on the set knew what was going on between the director and the leading lady. But for him to suddenly change the last scene of the movie? That was going to cost their small, undercapitalized, independent film more money. What on earth had he been thinking?

This wasn't like him. Lila had known Jason for almost ten years. She and her friend Erin had met him in film school. Lila truly hoped this sudden change had nothing to do with the new investor. Or with Erin's subdued mood.

No, if Erin knew something about the last-minute revisions, she would've passed it on. They'd been friends since the third grade. They told each other everything.

"Look, if my character ends up in the sequel, that shouldn't impact your role. You're only slated to be a supporting actress, after all. It'll be quite a break for someone like you."

Lila looked at Penelope with half her dark roots still showing and tried not to laugh. Sad, really. If Penelope didn't have a script in front of her, she was hopeless. Invariably she'd say something tactless or embarrassing.

"I'm not worried," Lila said, and dipped the brush into the dye solution. Frankly, it hadn't occurred to her. She was more concerned about making it home to spend the holidays with her family. "Has Jason mentioned anything about breaking for Christmas?"

Penelope checked her watch, ignoring Lila, as usual. "Would you hurry this up? I have a dinner date."

"Going to the diner?"

Penelope met her eyes in the mirror. Miracle of all miracles—she laughed, instead of looking as if all crew members were barely tolerable. "I honestly don't understand how anyone can live in this town."

"Oh, I don't know. The place has a certain charm." Lila meant it, even though she'd grown up in Southern California. The people in Blackfoot Falls were friendly, and of course curious.

Clearly Penelope interpreted the comment as sarcasm and mistook Lila for a kindred spirit. With a little smile, Penelope went back to reading the script changes.

Fine with Lila. She didn't want to make small talk. She preferred having the time to think. If she could finagle four days off, she could get home for Christmas. It wouldn't be easy. The round-trip drive would leave her with only a day and a half with the family. Flying was out of the question since she was almost broke.

The quick turnaround wasn't ideal, but it would be worth it. She'd already missed decorating the house with her mom and sister. Even though she knew that some people thought it was silly, not being with her family, everyone singing carols while they cooked Christmas dinner together, was unimaginable. Her brother's wife, Cheryl, had joined the tradition last year. For Lila, Christmas and home were synonymous.

Just as she applied more solution to Penelope's dark regrowth, a scream pierced the low hum of the crowd milling around outside.

People started yelling.

"What was that?" Penelope pushed to get up, then must've remembered what she looked like with her hair plastered to her head and sank down again.

"I don't know." Lila rushed to the window, couldn't see anything, so she went to the door.

"What is it?"

"I can't tell." Lila tried to see past a crowd of extras blocking her view. "Hold on a second." She pulled off the plastic gloves and took the three rickety steps, her beat-up Nikes touching the hard ground just as she heard the distressed neighs of a horse.

"Stand back, everyone. No one needs to get hurt." The man's deep, steady voice drifted in the chill air as smooth as fine, warm brandy.

"Right now, people." That was Erin, from somewhere in the direction of the catering truck. "Give him room."

Lila found a narrow gap in the crowd and pushed through.

A beautiful black horse reared and let out a high, extended whinny. He wasn't penned or tethered but cornered by a cowboy with longish dark hair, wearing a tan hat with the brim pulled low. The man threw a rope around the horse's neck, and the animal tossed its head and stamped the ground.

A collective murmur rose from the crowd.

"You know who that stallion belongs to?"

Lila turned to the unfamiliar voice behind her. But the older, bearded man wasn't talking to her.

"Nope," the guy next to him replied. He smiled at her and touched the brim of his hat. "Afternoon, ma'am."

They were probably locals hired as extras. Quite a few were standing by, waiting to be called for the next scene.

Lila returned his smile, then resumed watching the scene unfolding in front of her.

Moving in slowly, the cowboy whispered something to the horse. He didn't stop, just kept speaking in a low, hushed voice. Whatever it was, the stallion began to calm down.

"Is that Clint Landers? I think it is. I see his Whispering Pines trailer over there."

Lila shuddered. Partly because the stallion had a fierce look about him, but there was something about the tall, lean cowboy that had her wrapping her arms around herself to ward off another shiver.

Stepping aside, she turned to the two men. "Do you know what happened?"

"That black broke loose. Someone didn't tether him proper. He should've been left in the corral."

"What's the Whispering Pines?" she asked just as she spotted the white horse trailer.

"It's the Landers family's ranch," the bearded man said. "That fella with the stallion is Clint Landers."

Hmm. He looked to be in his early thirties. Probably married.

"Are you an actress?" The younger guy hadn't stopped staring at her.

"Not exactly," she said. "I do hair and makeup."

"Well, that's not right. You're too gorgeous not to be a movie star."

She just smiled and turned to watch the cowboy. She could've told him she was an actress. It was the truth.

She just wasn't acting in this particular film. But she'd played a few bit parts here and there, and soon enough she would make the transition from struggling wannabe to an honest-to-goodness, card-carrying member of the Screen Actors Guild. But lately, probably because of how tired she was, how tired everyone was, she wasn't quite as thrilled as she had been about her long-held dream.

The action had died down. The cowboy and the horse seemed to have reached an understanding, and the crowd started to thin.

Clint Landers.

Huh. For some reason she thought the name suited him. He was still talking to the animal in a hushed tone, and she stepped closer, wishing she could hear his voice again.

"Ma'am?"

She stopped and turned.

The bearded man had left, but the younger one, who was about her age, stood there, hat in hand. "My name is Brady." He had a great smile. "Sorry about sounding like a starstruck hayseed."

"I'm Lila," she said, but didn't extend her hand. It was too darn cold. Instead, she hugged herself tighter. "You paid me a compliment. I should have thanked you."

"Ah, no worries. You must hear stuff like that all the time."

She did, but she wasn't about to admit it, so she just smiled. After six years of trying to make it in this brutal business, she'd made peace with comments like his. But she had done nothing to earn her looks, and lucky for her, she'd been raised to believe praise was reserved for merit.

"Are you staying in town?" Brady asked.

"No. Most of us are camped out here." She spotted Erin and waved to get her attention. "I'm sorry, Brady, I'm actually working. Would you excuse me, please?"

"Sure." His smile faded as he stumbled back a step.

Erin walked up. "Are you an extra?" she asked him, and he nodded. "The director needs you on the set."

"Yes, ma'am. Bye, Lila. I hope to see you around," he said and jogged off.

"Yet another heart you've broken," Erin muttered, watching him for a moment. "He's cute."

"Yes. But the guy with the horse? Holy cow." Lila ignored her friend and watched Clint lead the horse toward the corrals. "I wonder if he's married?"

"Clint?" Erin gave her a long look. "Why, Lila Loveridge, I'm shocked. Are you interested in that cowboy?"

Lila frowned at her. "You know him?"

"Not really. I signed for some stock he's delivering. Seems like a nice guy. I was about to go thank him for saving our asses. Want to come with?" Erin's grin died as she looked past her. "What the hell is he doing?"

Lila saw right away that she meant Baxter, the new investor's nephew, with whom the crew was supposed to play nice. He was headed toward the corrals with a scowl on his pasty face. Another annoying person with an ego issue. He and Penelope would make a good—

Penelope.

Lila glanced toward the trailer. She'd completely forgotten about her. Tough. Erin was already on the move, and Lila wasn't going to miss this.

"I'm gonna kill him," Erin muttered, walking fast and glaring ahead as Baxter approached Clint.

"Please do. For everyone's sake."

Baxter was of average height, had a pudgy build and

apparently lacked enough sense to stay out of the much
taller man's face.

"Look, pal, if you can't control your animals, we'll
find a supplier who can." Baxter's loud warning reached
everyone within a five-yard radius, which was clearly
his intention.

Clint barely spared him a glance before turning back
to stroke the horse's neck, as if he'd never been interrupted. Without a word, he unlatched the corral gate.

"Baxter," Erin yelled. "Stop. Now."

Lila bit back a smile. He was no match for Erin, and
he knew it. In fact, Baxter was afraid of her. And he got
no sympathy whatsoever from Lila. In the week since
he'd joined the crew, he'd hit on her so many times, it
had gone from annoying to creepy.

Baxter shot them a nervous look, then took in the
group of curious bystanders. He squared his shoulders and again faced Clint, who was basically ignoring
everything around him while he got the horse safely
inside the empty corral.

"I'm so tempted to let the jerk get his lights punched
out," Erin said in a low voice as they approached the
two men. "It was Todd's fault the horse got loose, so
cool it, Baxter. The animal doesn't even belong to Mr.
Landers." Erin stopped, and Lila almost rammed into
her.

Up close, Clint Landers was even better looking.
Beard stubble darkened his square jaw and almost hid
the dimple in his chin. His bottom lip was considerably
fuller than his upper one, which appealed to Lila in a
big way. She worked with a lot of smoking hot guys,
but she couldn't recall the last time one of them made
her feel all tingly inside.

"We're damn lucky he was there," Erin was saying.

The smile she'd given Clint vanished as she switched her focus to Baxter. "We owe him our thanks, and an apology from you."

Baxter's pale face flamed.

Erin wouldn't give an inch. Her glare narrowed meaningfully. Advising everyone to play nice excluded her and Jason.

"Hey, it was an honest mistake," Clint said, making sure the gate was latched before pulling off a leather work glove and extending his hand to Baxter. "No harm done."

Baxter hesitated, clearly unwilling to give in. But it was equally clear that he had no choice. What an idiot.

He made sure everyone watching caught his condescending smirk before he stuck out his hand. Clint clasped it and gave Baxter a couple of firm pumps. Baxter looked as though he was about to choke. If his face had been red before, now it was turning scarlet.

Clint pumped his hand a couple more times. "No hard feelings...pal," he said with a big smile and released Baxter's hand.

He immediately flexed it, while subtly trying to draw in some air.

"I don't think anything's broken," Erin said with a straight face.

Lila pressed her lips together and quickly turned her head. And met Clint Landers's eyes. They were brown. Light brown with gold flecks. And he had thick dark lashes that took nothing away from his rugged good looks.

The man was positively dreamy.

She needed a little air herself. But she managed to give him a smile without hyperventilating.

"Clint Landers," he said in the same deep, velvety tone he'd used with the stallion.

"Lila Loveridge." She stared down at his extended, bone-crushing hand. "Um, I don't think so."

"Come on," he said, amusement curving his mouth in a slow smile. "Live dangerously."

With a laugh, she dragged a palm down her jeans before letting his large hand engulf hers. His grip was firm, yet gentle. He was the real deal. A genuine cowboy who did physical labor, and with rough, callused palms to prove it. And those muscled arms and shoulders? Not bulk, just lean muscle. Oh yeah, he looked darn fine.

And the other thing about him—he had no problem looking a person directly in the eyes.

"Nice to meet you," she said, pulling back her hand and lowering her gaze to his chest. "You're wearing a T-shirt."

He glanced down. "I am."

Lila sighed. "It's December." Why did the really hot guys always have to be crazy? "And it's freezing."

"Also true." He glanced at the horse. "I was changing in my truck when this guy here decided to make a break for it." He held out his hand and the horse nuzzled it. "You know if he belongs to Ben Wolf?"

"No, I don't." She turned to ask Erin, but one of Jason's flunkies had pulled her and Baxter aside and was whispering something to the two of them.

Whatever it was, Baxter stopped glaring at her and Clint and gave the young man a sharp look. Then he turned toward the set, where Jason was setting up the next shot. His uncle expected a big return on his investment, and Jason's word was gospel. The project's success trumped Baxter's self-importance. It had to.

"Who's in charge of looking after the stock?" Clint's gaze flicked to Baxter. "Not that guy, I hope," he added in a lowered voice, looking back at her.

"Oh, God, no. That would be Charlie. He's the head wrangler, and he's very responsible. I haven't seen him today, but he should be around... Older guy. White hair. Wears it in a ponytail." She thought Charlie might be in town, but she glanced around anyway, because staring into Clint's eyes made it hard to concentrate on anything but him. "I don't see him. We haven't had any other incidents with animals getting loose, though."

"I'd like to speak with him before unloading my trailer."

"Erin should know where he is." Lila gestured vaguely, noticing that someone else now had her friend's ear. Fine with Lila. It gave her more time to check out Clint. "She shouldn't be long."

"I'm in no hurry." He lifted his hat and swept back a long dark lock of hair before settling the brim low on his forehead.

"Are you also an extra?"

"An extra what?"

"I guess not." She smiled. "You said you were changing your shirt so I thought... We hire local people to be in the movie."

"You're kidding."

"Most people like it. They don't say any lines and it pays practically nothing, but they get bragging rights. Hey, if you're interested—"

"No," he said quickly. "No. No way. Not me."

"You can't be camera shy."

He laughed. "Thanks anyway."

Lila jumped when someone touched her shoulder.

She instinctively recoiled when she saw it was Baxter, but then put on a neutral smile. Some actress she was.

"I need to talk to Mr. Landers," he said with an obvious lack of enthusiasm.

She looked at Erin who now stood alone, motioning with her head for Lila to join her.

Glancing back at Clint, it was all Lila could do not to sigh. "Well, nice meeting you," she said and realized she'd already mentioned something to that effect.

They exchanged smiles, and he politely touched the brim of his hat. But it was the dark penetrating look in his eyes that had her heart pounding as she turned and hurried the short distance to Erin.

"Come on," Erin said with a little smile and started walking toward the trailers that were lined up out of camera range.

"What does Baxter want with him, and where are we going?"

"You're wearing a T-shirt? Seriously?"

Lila looked at her, and Erin burst out laughing.

"Shut up." Lila shook her head and then laughed, too.

"On a shitty note, Penelope is on the warpath."

"Oh. Right. I forgot about her." God, Lila was tempted to look back at him.

"No. Hell, no." Clint's voice had raised some.

Lila and Erin looked at each other, and then they both turned to see him walking away from Baxter, who stared daggers after him. Whatever it was the creep wanted, Lila doubted it was a face full of dust kicked up by Clint's boots as he strode toward his horse trailer.

"What was that about?" Lila asked.

"Jason wants to use Clint in his next scene and said he wouldn't take no for an answer," she said absently.

As Erin continued to stare at Baxter, Lila could almost see the wheels turning in her friend's head. She and Jason's new flunky hadn't gotten along from day one. Baxter was green and unfamiliar with the film industry, while Erin knew just about everything there was to know.

Since college she'd worked nearly every job there was behind the camera. She was supposed to be showing Baxter the ropes, which was probably why she'd been so grumpy lately.

This project was important for their future in the industry. Just like Lila, Erin's big chance was coming up with the sequel. She'd been promised the first assistant director's job.

"I know you," Lila said. "You're planning something evil."

Erin smiled. "Who was it that said 'the enemy of my enemy is my friend'?"

Lila's gaze went to Clint, his back to them as he pulled on a long-sleeve shirt. "Friend? Oh, I want him for so much more than that."

2

CLINT PARKED HIS truck close to the circular drive in front of his brother's house. He got out and lifted a hand to Woody, the foreman, and a pair of Lucky 7 hired men walking toward the bunkhouse. The air was chilly, but he didn't bother grabbing his jacket since it was a short walk to the fancy wrought-iron gate. He couldn't stay long, but he had time to kill and something he wanted to get off his chest. Nathan was always a good sounding board.

After letting himself into the small courtyard, he went straight to the front door and wiped the bottoms of his boots on the mat. He rang the bell, glancing around while he waited.

The place looked nice. Even with winter threatening to roll in with a bang, his sister-in-law had spruced up the courtyard with Christmas wreaths and garland. Strings of lights were draped along the stone archway and wrapped around the porch columns.

He liked Beth a lot and not just because she'd been so good for Nathan, bringing him back to life after his first wife's death. Clint admired Beth for leaving small remembrances of Anne, like her prized roses and topiary garden. Anne had liked everything manicured and perfect, and Beth was the total opposite.

The door opened. "Hey, I didn't know you were coming over," Beth said, stepping back to let him inside.

"Yeah, I should've called first."

"Oh, please. You know better. Nathan's in his office, and I was just putting up some Christmas decorations."

Clint smelled coffee as he walked into the large foyer. Pinecones and conifer branches littered the cherry console table. A ball of string had fallen to the hardwood floor. He scooped it up and gave it to Beth.

"I decided to make my own wreaths." She rolled her eyes. "I won't make that mistake again."

"I just came from Blackfoot Falls. I saw you have the inn all decked out. It looks nice."

"Really? You don't think I went overboard?" she asked, frowning and swiping back wisps of blond hair from her eyes.

His thoughts shot straight to Lila. Not a shocker. He hadn't been able to shake the image of her the whole ride over. Her hair was a lighter shade of blond than Beth's, and Lila's eyes were blue, a real cornflower blue you just didn't see every day. She was a stunner, the most beautiful woman he'd ever seen in person. Or more like ever. He'd never been a moviegoer or had much time for TV, but if he'd seen her starring in anything, he would've remembered.

"I did, didn't I?" Beth was staring at him. "Was it the lighted Happy Holidays sign? I worried that might be a bit much."

He frowned, then recalled they'd been talking about the old boardinghouse Beth had bought and converted to an inn. "No," he said. "It looks nice. Very festive.

Sorry, I was thinking about that coffee I smell. Any chance—"

Beth laughed. "Of course. Help yourself."

Clint continued into the kitchen, poured a mug of the strong brew and took it with him to his brother's office down the hall. The door was open. Nathan was sitting at his desk working on his laptop.

"Hey, got a minute?"

Nathan looked up. "I thought I heard your voice. Everything okay?"

"Hell, it hasn't been that long since I've visited." Clint settled in the brown leather chair across from his brother.

"Yeah, but in the middle of a weekday?"

"You got me there."

Nathan's cell rang, and Clint gestured for him to go ahead and answer. It dawned on him that he wasn't exactly sure what he wanted to say. Or even how to broach the subject without sounding as if he was complaining.

Naturally the call was short—bought him all of five seconds.

Clint took a slow sip of coffee, then cradled the warm mug in his hands. "I got the talk from Dad last night."

Nathan's eyes narrowed. "Did you tell him you already know storks have nothing to do with it?"

"Hell, no. I'm not sure he and Mom have figured it out yet."

"They have three grown sons. I think they might've put two-and-two together by now."

"Stop." Clint shook his head. "There are some things a man just can't ponder. No matter how old he is."

"Amen to that. So, last night, was Seth there, too?"

"He's still in Billings."

"Partying with his old college buddies?" Nathan's

expression hardened when Clint shrugged. "When does Dad want you to take over?"

"Soon. He'd like an answer by Christmas."

His brother's brows shot up, but he quickly masked his surprise. It didn't matter. Clint knew Nathan had expected him to run Whispering Pines eventually. Everyone did. The ranch had survived everything from droughts to poor financial management to be passed down through five generations of Landerses.

Nathan was two years older and a hard act to follow. He'd begun building the Lucky 7 from practically nothing while he was still in college. And now, at thirty-five, he owned one of the most profitable ranches in the county.

"Did Dad tell you to think about it? Or was that your suggestion?"

"It was mutual. He told me to take some time off, to really think. I don't see Seth wanting any part of it. Do you?"

Nathan shook his head. "Hell, I don't know what's going on with that kid."

"He's almost thirty."

"And acting like he's ten."

Clint rubbed his jaw. Man, he needed a shave. "Think it's time for his two big brothers to have a sit-down with him?"

"Maybe after the holidays. We don't want to stir things up and ruin Christmas for Mom."

"Good point."

"I'm more concerned about you right now."

"Me?"

Nathan was studying him a little too closely. "You're not jumping at the chance to take over—" He held up a hand. "And I'm not saying you should. After you quit college, I guess I just assumed you missed ranching."

"So did I, but…" Clint hesitated. Damn, he should've thought this thing through. Not five minutes ago he'd realized he wasn't prepared. He could've talked about the weather, the Denver Broncos making it to the playoffs, the price of alfalfa… The last thing he wanted was to make Nathan feel guilty for breaking tradition. The oldest son had always taken the reins. But that didn't mean anything.

Yep, Clint should've waited. Although the talk with his dad had completely caught him off guard, and he'd been having trouble thinking straight, or about anything else—that was until he'd met Lila.

"Did you ever think about doing anything other than ranching?"

Nathan leaned back in his chair. "No, I haven't. But clearly you have."

"No. Well, nothing specific. It's just getting pretty real is all. It's a damn serious commitment."

"Hell, you've been in charge since before Dad made you foreman," Nathan said. "The men go to you when they need something, and we both know Dad likes it that way. Making it official won't change much. Unless there's something else you're not saying?"

"That's just it. I don't feel as though I'd be losing out on anything, but I don't want to just slide in because it's what's expected of me either. On the other hand, if I don't step up and Dad were to get sick again, or if Seth doesn't come around and start pulling his weight, I'd feel like shit."

"I understand," Nathan said. "So would I, but it didn't stop me from building the ranch I wanted."

Clint just nodded, but that was the difference between

him and Nathan. His brother had always known what he wanted, and Clint wasn't sure. He still loved ranching, and it would kill him if anyone but a Landers owned the land. Wasn't that enough reason for him to step up? He'd never been commitment-phobic, so why was the thought of sealing his future making him twitchy?

"Sorry to interrupt." Beth poked her head in. "I'm going to run into town for some ribbon. Do you need anything?"

"Blackfoot Falls or Twin Creeks?" Nathan asked with an amused gleam in his eye. Twin Creeks was closer to the Lucky 7 but half the size of Blackfoot Falls.

"Oh, please... Blackfoot Falls, of course. Who knows?" She batted her lashes. "I might get discovered."

Clint shot a look at his brother. The night Anne had died in the accident, she'd sneaked off to audition for a play.

Nathan didn't seem bothered, he just laughed. "Well, you call me before you sign any contracts."

"Deal," she said, padding in to give him a quick kiss. "Text me if you think of anything you want." On her way out, she squeezed Clint's shoulder. "We're having chicken and tortilla casserole for supper if you want to stay."

"Thanks. Another time." The second she was out of earshot Clint grinned at his brother. "She's got you eating casseroles?"

Grunting, Nathan leaned back. "Wait till you get married. You're gonna find yourself doing a lot of crap you swore you wouldn't do. Hey, you still seeing Kristy?"

"Not for months. It wasn't going anywhere." He shrugged. "I think she might have itchy feet. Wouldn't surprise me if she moved away from Twin Creeks."

"Is that what's got you hesitating to take over from Dad?"

"Nah." Clint shook his head for emphasis. "Anyway, it's nothing. Just thinking things through."

"You guys having any financial problems I should know about?"

"Nope." It was a fair question. Years ago their father had made some poor decisions that had nearly bankrupted them. "We're in the black."

"Thanks to you," Nathan said, his worried pucker beginning to ease. "But I heard you leased horses to the Hollywood people, so it made me wonder."

"Didn't do it for the money. Ben Wolf asked me for a favor. They wanted a couple of showy chestnuts. We have geldings with cream-colored manes and tails that fit the bill." Clint had unloaded the horses without talking to the head wrangler. For some reason, he'd trusted Erin Murphy's word the runaway stallion was an isolated incident. But he had every intention of driving back later to make sure they weren't being careless with the animals. "You ever heard of Lila Loveridge?"

Nathan frowned. "Nope. She live around here?"

Clint wished. "She's an actress. Blonde. About five-eight. I just met her. You and Beth watch more movies than I do, so I figured you might've seen her in something."

"I can look her up," Nathan said, straightening and reaching for his laptop.

"Nah." Hell, he should've thought of that himself. "She's so far out of my league, it isn't funny."

Even before seeing Nathan's startled look, Clint regretted the stupid remark. What a dumb-ass thing to say. He'd just made idle curiosity sound like it was a big deal.

Jesus.

"Some jerk asked if I wanted to be in the movie. I wouldn't have to say anything. Just stand next to a horse and look like a jackass."

Nathan grinned. "What did you say?"

"What do you think?"

Lucky for him, his brother's phone rang.

Clint stood. Perfect time to make an exit.

Glancing at the cell, Nathan said, "Sit. It's only Woody."

"I've got to go." Clint glanced at his watch and started for the door. "We'll talk another time."

"You sure you don't wanna stay for some of Beth's casserole? I guarantee she made plenty."

Clint laughed. "I heard leftovers are even better the next day," he said on his way out of the office, grinning when he heard his brother curse.

Despite Erin's assurance, Clint figured he'd go see if the head wrangler had showed up. Although if he was being honest, he wanted to see Lila again.

THE SUN HADN'T dipped behind the Rockies yet, but the sky was overcast, which meant it would get dark early. Everyone was rushing to make use of the daylight and making more mistakes. It was just one of those days. Lots of small, annoying things had gone wrong, and everyone seemed to be on edge. The two bars in town would likely be hopping tonight.

Lila wasn't much of a drinker, but even she was considering a trip into town with everyone else. A beer shouldn't cost too much.

She watched an older man transfer his chew of tobacco from one cheek to the other, and managed not to cringe. Disgusting. In the three months she'd been working on location in cattle country, she'd grown used to many unfamiliar customs. But chewing tobacco? Yuck.

The man was an extra, not an actor, but they were using him for several close-ups during the bar-fight scene. So Lila had been called to the set to make sure his fake injuries were consistent for each shot.

Initially she'd been in charge of hair, and hadn't done much makeup. But she'd been learning a lot, and she liked having the variety, so she never minded pitching in when they asked for her.

"You need to make the scar longer," Erin said, studying the photo and then the man's jaw. "Bring it closer to his ear."

"I'm back." Glenda, an intern, showed up to take over.

"Let Lila finish the scar and then—" Erin glared at the man. "Would you stop chewing?"

He stopped.

Lila and Glenda exchanged private smiles. Erin was their hero. She was never mean or petty, but if someone wanted to be coddled, they'd better look elsewhere.

Every film needed someone as smart and efficient as Erin. Especially a low-budget, indy project like this one. So much was riding on it for a lot of people—including her and Erin. The film's success could make their careers. Or conversely, bankrupt them. The two of them were low-level investors, but it had taken every penny they'd saved, every favor owed them, and they'd even taken out small loans. Lila tried not to think about that too much. It made her queasy.

She quickly went to work on the man's scar, and just as she applied the finishing touch, Erin said, "Guess who's back?"

Lila's pulse quickened. "Shut. The. Front. Door," she said, staring at her friend. Erin's teasing smile was a big hint. Had to be the cowboy Lila had been daydreaming about all afternoon. "Are you serious?"

"As a heart attack. But don't turn—" Erin sighed when Lila whipped around for a look.

"Where?" A black truck parked near the corrals hadn't been there ten minutes ago. No sign of Clint, though. "Is he—oh, crap," she muttered when she caught sight of Baxter.

Erin's expression changed completely when she saw him hurrying toward them. "What do you want?"

"That guy...Landers." Baxter was out of breath. "He's back."

"So?"

"Jason wants to use him tomorrow." Baxter was so clueless. Whatever it was he wanted, his haughty tone wasn't going to win Erin over.

"Need anything else, Erin?" Glenda asked, already backing away.

"Nope. We're good for now."

"You have to go talk to Landers," Baxter said. "Jason insists that—"

"Jason told *you* to do it. Lila, got a minute?" Erin started walking toward the set, and Lila went along with her.

"Yeah, but—" Baxter's face flushed.

Erin stopped. "But what? Landers told you to take a hike?"

Baxter's defiant glare faded. "I don't get why Jason has to have *him*."

"Well, that's a problem. You should be *getting it*. You need to understand those small details if you want to—"

Erin cut herself short. She blinked, thought a few seconds and tried to hold back a smile. "Ask Lila to do it."

Baxter's mouth tightened. It was obvious he didn't like that idea. Finally he turned to her. "Will you talk to Landers?"

"Maybe." Lila let him stew while she willed her pulse to slow down. "Okay, I'll do it. But you'll owe me."

Baxter had the nerve to look smug again.

Lila jabbed a finger at him. "Owe me big. Got it?"

Baxter grinned. "I'll take you to dinner in Kalispell."

She could only stare at him. Clearly he was insane.

"Oh." A smile brightened Erin's face. "Spencer's here."

Lila turned and waved. She really liked Spencer, and was thrilled Erin had found love and the deep sense of contentment he'd provided in her life. Knowing that helped Lila ignore the occasional pang of jealousy. Over not having someone to share a pillow with at night. Or be there to listen to the highs and lows of her day. And she missed having Erin around all the time.

"Do you mind if I leave?" Erin asked, watching her closely. "Have you got this?"

Lila gave her a big smile. "Oh yeah."

"There he is," Baxter said, peering in the direction of the corrals. "Landers."

"Big," Lila reminded him as she walked backward. "And no dinner." She turned toward Clint and hurried her pace when she saw him and Charlie shake hands.

If he went for his truck, she'd head him off.

She didn't have to do anything but keep walking. The moment Clint saw her, he stopped.

"Hey," she said, wishing she'd changed her big sloppy sweatshirt for something nicer.

"Hello again."

"I see you found Charlie."

Clint nodded. "Nice guy. Knows horses."

"That's what I've heard. Me, I don't know anything about… I saw your chestnuts."

He blinked, and it might have been a trick of the light, but his face darkened.

"Um, geldings? Horses?"

"Right. Sure."

"Did I say that wrong?"

"No." He shook his head. "I knew exactly what you meant." His gaze drifted toward the set. "You all work late every night?"

"Only when we're shooting a night scene."

Clint chuckled. "I'm sure I'll have a few more dumb questions."

Lila smiled. She liked having to tilt her head back to look at him. "You want to ask them over a beer?"

He met her eyes. His jaw clenched.

"Unless you need to get home for dinner," she said quickly. "Your wife and kids might be waiting." She paused long enough for him to deny it, but he didn't. "I'm supposed to convince you to be in the movie. So, you know, it's not personal or anything."

He actually looked disappointed. "That's a shame," he said, his mouth quirking upward. "Since I don't have a wife or kids."

"No?" She cleared her throat. "Then how about that beer?"

3

THE FULL MOON SALOON had opened in July, but this was Clint's first time in the place. He'd heard about the mechanical bull in the back and shouldn't have been surprised by the small dance floor, since he knew a live band played Friday and Sunday nights. The only music now was something by Keith Urban coming from the jukebox.

It wasn't too crowded yet. Some guys were shooting pool in the back, and half the stools at the bar were occupied by local cowboys. Clint nodded at two men he recognized from the Circle K. They nodded back, but their eyes were on Lila. That was probably true for just about every guy in the room.

"Table or bar?" he asked her, hoping she'd choose a table so they could have some privacy.

"How about that one?" she said, gesturing toward a nice corner table.

"After you."

She led the way, and he did his damnedest not to stare at her behind. Not that he could see much anyway. It looked like she'd worn the same jeans, but she'd traded the old sweatshirt he'd assumed went with whatever role she was playing, for another that was just as bulky.

She pulled out a chair that had her facing the wall. "It's going to get busy in here," she said as she settled gracefully in her seat. "I saw two stuntmen playing pool. They won't bother us, but you can bet someone from the crew will invite himself over eventually."

Clint took the chair across the table from her. Sitting with her back to the room wouldn't matter. No man with eyes in his head would be able to pass her by without a second or third look.

"I just realized something," she said with a laugh. "This is a small town. It's kind of like a big film crew where people think nothing of pulling up a chair whether you're having a private conversation or not."

"Yep, that's about the size of it."

"Shall we make a bet on whose people will interrupt us first?"

"To be clear, the waitress doesn't count, right?" He grinned at her puzzled expression.

Lila turned just as Elaine got to their table.

"Good Lord. Clint Landers." The short brunette stuck a pencil behind her ear and put a hand on her hip. "How long has it been since I've laid eyes on you?"

"It's been a while."

"Not since Anne's…" Elaine glanced at Lila and smiled.

"I think you're right," Clint said, hoping to ease the sudden awkwardness. "It was at Anne's funeral. Hard to believe it's been four years."

Elaine nodded. "I've seen Nathan a few times. He looks good. I didn't get to talk to him, though, so tell him I said hey."

"Will do."

"Well, what can I get you folks?"

Lila surprised him once again by ordering a draft beer. He told Elaine to make it two, and was about to introduce the women when another customer called for Elaine.

As soon as she left, Lila said, "Okay, I must have a serious misconception of a small town."

"You think we all know each other?"

"Yes, that, too, but how can you go four years without seeing someone?"

"Salina is a big county, and the ranches are all spread out. I don't come to Blackfoot Falls all that much, and when I do it's usually to pick up something at the hardware store. And since I live across the county line, I went to a different school than most of the folks around here."

"But you've lived in the area your whole life?"

"Other than two years of college, yeah."

"Your family is still here?"

Clint nodded and skipped the part that he still lived in the family home, sleeping in the same room he had as a kid. Sometimes it bothered him, even though it was a common practice with families who owned big ranches. But today the idea stuck in his craw.

"Do you have brothers and sisters? Nieces and nephews?" she asked, and seemed genuinely interested. She wasn't being nosy or making small talk.

"Two brothers. Nathan is older than me. Seth is younger and a real pain in the butt."

Lila laughed. "I have one of those, too," she said with a wistful sigh. "Oh, I guess Britney isn't that bad. She started college this fall and is feeling overwhelmed by life in general. But we talk a lot."

"You miss her."

"Yes. I miss everybody—my parents and brother, his wife. They all live in California where I grew up. These last three months are the longest I've ever been away from them."

Clint could just stare at her all night. She had an expressive face and skin as fine as his mother's bone china. Right now, that face was telling him he'd missed a cue.

Shit.

He cleared his throat. "I would think you travel a lot."

"Not really. And certainly not for this long. We're behind schedule. I'm not sure what will happen at Christmas."

"You mean you won't have the day off?"

"Oh, we will. Thanks to the unions. But I don't know that any of us are going to have enough time to make it home." She shrugged, as if it wasn't a big deal, and smiled at Elaine as she set down two foamy mugs.

"I'll start a tab for you folks, yes?" Elaine said.

Clint was about to agree when Lila shook her head. She dug into her pocket. "What do I owe you?"

"Elaine, I've got this." He pulled out a twenty at the same time Lila produced a handful of crumpled bills.

"I asked you to come, so my treat," she said, busy trying to straighten her money. "In fact I'm going to make Baxter reimburse me."

Clint slipped Elaine the twenty, and she quietly left to make change.

Lila looked up and twisted in her seat. "Where'd she go?"

A group who had to be movie people had just entered the bar. The short stocky guy leading the pack spotted Lila right away.

She acknowledged the hand he lifted, sighing as she

turned back to face Clint. "I thought we'd have more time before the troops descended."

"You want to leave?"

"No. Maybe they'll play pool. But if they come over, then…"

"I won't have any trouble getting rid of them," Clint said, and she gave him a peculiar smile. "If that's what you want."

"Wait. Did Elaine take your money?"

"Look, I'll be honest with you." He leaned forward. "I had to pay the check. Because I'm going to brag like hell that I had a date with a bona fide movie star, and it wouldn't be a date if I didn't pay, now would it?"

Arching her brows, she laughed softly.

"I won't use your name if you don't want me to."

"I can't tell if you're serious."

"I am." Clint looked into her pretty blue eyes and had an almost uncontrollable urge to lean closer and kiss her. He was likely to clear the whole damn table trying, but he might be willing…

"One problem." She picked up her mug and took a tiny sip. "I'm not a movie star."

"What do you mean? You're an actress, right?"

"Yes and no." Lila shrugged. "I've done shampoo commercials, and I've had tiny parts in a few TV movies. But I do have a good shot at a decent role coming up."

Clint frowned. Something didn't add up.

"Sorry to disappoint you."

"I'm not…disappointed. Just confused."

"I'm part of the crew, working as a hairstylist. And I do some makeup, too. It's a small independent movie and we're operating on a shoestring, so our jobs tend to overlap."

"But acting isn't one of yours?"

"Not for this project. But I've wanted to be an actress since I was a kid. I even went to UCLA drama school." She smiled with that same wistfulness he'd heard in her voice earlier. "Along with fifty million other wannabes. It's a tough business to break into."

Clint opened his mouth, then realized he was about to say something totally stupid.

"What?"

He shook his head.

"Come on, you've got me curious."

"I'll just say that you look like a movie star. So you've already got that part down pat."

Lila laughed. "Well, thank you," she said with a slight nod. "I'll let my parents know you approve."

Clint ducked his head. He knew he should've kept his mouth shut.

"No, don't." Lila reached across the table and touched his hand. "I wasn't being snotty or sarcastic. I promise. It's just—"

He stared at her slim pale fingers resting on top of his big, rough ones, brown like leather from working in the hot sun. Her skin was soft, her touch so light it felt like a butterfly had landed on him. She withdrew her hand, and he looked up, wishing she hadn't.

"It's just…" she began again. "In this business it's important to keep things in perspective. My looks don't define me. I can't let them or I'll end up—" Lila blushed. "Oh, jeez. I can't believe I'm telling you all this stuff." She took a hasty sip of beer and made a face. Coughed a little. Muttered something about sticking to iced tea. And coughed again.

Clint hid a smile behind his mug, drinking his beer and giving her time to recover. She thought he was disappointed that she wasn't a movie star. Not even close. It wasn't that he thought he had a chance with her. He'd be a damn fool to think she'd go for a guy like him, some hick steeped in family tradition and the routine of ranch life. But he really admired her for not using her beauty as a crutch.

She stopped coughing, pushed the beer aside and looked at him while dabbing her watery eyes.

"I saw a sign for sarsaparillas. Only two bits," he said. "Maybe we can order you one of those."

"Very funny." With a cute little smile, she leaned forward as if she had a secret to tell him. "I'll admit I'm an umbrella drink kind of girl. And if the drink is pink or blue, that's even better."

"Elaine's on her way back. Let's see what we can do about that."

"No. I can't," Lila said, laughing. "I have to get up early tomorrow."

"Okay, then, when's your day off?" He saw her smile slip and knew he'd overstepped.

This was just part of the job for her. Have a beer with him, convince him to be the silent cowboy standing around like a jackass. Yeah, no way that was going to happen.

He watched more people come through the front door—three men, and a woman with purple hair, all in their twenties, looking a lot like they needed to let off some steam. They sure weren't locals.

"Sunday," Lila said. "I'm off on Sundays. Everyone is. You know, union rules and all."

Clint had no idea how unions operated. He knew a whole lot about ranching and raising cattle. But that was it. So why had he thought about asking her to go out with him? He'd bore her to death.

"How are you two doing?" Elaine laid his change on the table. "Can I get you anything else?"

Lila smiled and shook her head.

"No, thanks, Elaine. This is it for me."

"Well, good seeing you, Clint. You take care." Elaine gave Lila a parting nod and a lingering inspection as she went to the next table.

Lila was staring at him with a furrowed brow. "I know Sundays are usually family days, so I'm guessing it won't work for you."

Clint's heart lurched. He took another gulp of beer and discreetly wiped his mouth. Hell, he hoped he wasn't misreading her. "Sunday is fine. So is Saturday night—"

"I knew it was you hiding in the corner." A guy with tattoos on his neck came up behind Lila and tugged on her ponytail. "Can't miss this hair."

She swatted his hand away just as the rest of the group converged on them.

"Have you seen Rocco?" the woman with the purple hair asked as she strained to see into the back room.

"You know if they fixed the mechanical bull yet?" a younger guy muttered without looking up from his phone.

The fourth member of the party, a tall, clean-cut man stared at Clint.

Lila huffed with annoyance. "Everybody be quiet," she said, briefly closing her eyes before glancing up at them. "Did any of you stop for one second to wonder if you might be interrupting something here?"

The three people—who weren't sizing up Clint— looked at Lila and then looked at one another. "Nah," they said at once and grinned.

"Well, you are. I'm on a date. So butt out."

They all stared at her. Even Mr. Clean-cut dragged his gaze away from Clint to gape at Lila.

Clint just kept his mouth shut.

"No, you aren't," the tattooed guy said. "You never hook up. With anybody."

"Ever." The kid had lowered his phone.

"You don't hook up, and you don't cuss. Everyone knows that."

"Goodbye, Randy," Lila said to him with a shooing motion. "And Tony. Rhonda. Davis. Goodbye. See you all tomorrow."

Rhonda gave Clint a considering look, smiled and strolled off toward the bar.

"I mean it, you guys." Lila glared at the other three when they didn't budge. "Leave."

Clint reached across the table for her hand. The softness of her skin stunned him all over again. "How about *we* leave instead?"

"Yes. Even better."

He didn't want to let go of her hand, and she wasn't trying to pull away. Her smile lit him up inside. All the way down to the deepest, darkest pit where he stuffed feelings he didn't know what to do with.

Her fingers curled lightly around his. "Ready?"

Clearing his throat, he nodded and released her hand. He scraped back in his chair and noticed the guy who'd been staring at him hadn't gone far. Lila had called him Davis. His glare had been replaced with an obnoxious smirk. Probably thinking, *you poor dumb bastard.*

Clint got that, and he could live with it. At least for tonight, and if he was really lucky, Saturday night too.

4

"SORRY ABOUT THAT," Lila said once they were sitting in his truck. "Film crews should never be released into the general population. They have no manners. No sense of—"

Clint started the engine and glanced over at her, an amused expression on his face.

"Yes, I know I'm one of them," she continued. "But I do have manners."

"They didn't bother me," he said with a laugh. "But I can't say I was sorry to get out of there, either."

"And what I said about us being on a date... I hope that didn't upset you."

"Lila." He let the truck idle and turned to look at her. "Do you honestly think I would care if anyone assumed we were on a date?"

"I don't know. If you had a girlfriend, you would." She paused, waiting for him to respond. "You don't, right?"

"No, I don't have a girlfriend. If you're free Saturday night, would you like to have dinner with me?"

"Yes."

"Good." He started to put the truck in gear but cut

the engine instead. "One more thing," he said, and leaned over the console.

His hand slipped behind her neck as he pressed his mouth against hers. Startled, her lips parted on a silent gasp. But he didn't mistake her reaction for an invitation and rush in. He took his time, his mouth warm and firm as it moved over hers, his large hand cupping her nape. His fingers exerted a slight pressure, just enough to make her ache for more of his touch.

She parted her lips a little more. His tongue slipped inside, teasing, tasting, probing, then retreated too soon. Clint just stopped kissing her and leaned back. She didn't understand what had just happened, then relaxed as a lazy smile curved his mouth.

"I could kiss you all night," he whispered, brushing the back of his hand down her cheek.

"I didn't stop you," she said, hoping the semidarkness hid her blush.

"No, I have to keep myself in check before I—get carried away." He toyed with her hair, letting a tendril curl around his finger. "I have manners, too."

She loved the smell of him. His scent was warm and musky and very masculine in a way she couldn't describe. There was a hint of soap, maybe leather, and a big helping of easygoing confidence.

"Why don't you date?"

"I don't meet many men outside the industry. And hooking up with coworkers rarely turns out well. I won't do it. People gossip about nothing as it is. I refuse to feed them anything they can distort. I'm not thick-skinned enough." She saw that he was really listening and maybe having trouble making sense of what she was telling him. "And yes, to be in this business I need to be tougher. I know that, and hopefully I'll get there."

Clint frowned, withdrawing his hand. "That would be a shame. From what I've seen, you're already firm and assertive. You don't let anyone bulldoze you. I think you're plenty tough."

"Oh, you don't know this business," she said, laughing.

"You're right. I don't know the first thing about it. What I do know is that I like you just the way you are."

Lila searched his eyes. It could've been just a line, but it didn't feel like that. "I mean, how often do you hear the word *date* anymore? Nowadays, if you even hear the word, it's usually a euphemism for sex."

"I seem to recall us both using it. That's not what I meant."

She couldn't help grinning at his offended expression. "I didn't think you did, not for a second. If I had, we wouldn't be having this conversation."

"See?" The skin at the outside corner of his eyes crinkled with humor. "You can be tough."

Lila had forgotten what a joy it was to be talking with a man she liked, who had no association with Hollywood. No hidden agendas. She had a feeling that with Clint, what you saw was exactly what you got. "By the way, I do cuss. A lot." She moved her hand to rest on his. "But only in my head." Clint laughed just as she was about to lean forward and show him how assertive she could be. "Hey," she murmured, "that counts."

"You're right." His voice had lowered, and his gaze dropped to her mouth. "We should go someplace."

"Where?"

"Anywhere but here." His flat tone prompted her to follow his gaze.

Two men were crossing Main Street, but she didn't know them.

"Have you eaten?" Clint asked. "We can grab something quick at the diner, or if you have time, there's a new steak house—"

"Sorry, I can't." She sat back. "I was teasing earlier. We do film at night, indoor scenes, especially when we're this far behind schedule. They might need me later, but I won't know until the last minute."

"Ah, but you haven't convinced me to be an extra. So your job here isn't done yet."

"That's true." She fastened her seat belt when he started the engine.

"Hey, who's that Baxter character, anyway?"

Lila sighed. "A pain in everyone's behind, but he has a rich uncle who's written us a big fat check, and now everyone has to put up with him."

"You mean the guy's in charge?"

"Oh, God, no. Baxter's just the director's glorified errand boy. He's supposed to be learning the business."

"So he gets chewed out if I don't want to be an extra? Not you. Is that right?"

"Oh, I have nothing to do with it. If you had agreed, then Baxter would owe me. That's all."

"I noticed a bunch of local cowboys standing around. I assume they've been hired. Why not use one of them?"

"If Jason, the director, sees something he wants in a particular shot, he won't let it go. Whether it's a person or a storefront or a mountain, he gets obsessed. He and Erin went to war over using Moonlight Mountain. Do you know it?"

"Sure. Who won?"

"Erin." Lila grinned like a proud mama, which made Clint laugh.

She was guessing that the way he'd handled the runaway horse, shutting out everything around him, his focus laser sharp until it was just him and the stallion, was what had drawn Jason's attention.

As they drove down Main Street, she studied Clint's profile, seeing him just as the camera would see him.

With his strong stubbled jaw and intense gaze, he was the quintessential cowboy hero. On the other hand, she could just as easily picture him as an outlaw, his face on an old West wanted poster. Either way the camera would love him.

"You know what, it might be fun," she said. "Something different."

"What?"

"Being in the film. It's not like learning a role. But I should point out that while you'd be considered an extra, you won't be just a face in the crowd like the others. The director will want some close-ups and shots of you standing alone, apart from the action. A shadowy red herring."

Clint looked at her as if she'd forgotten to brush her teeth.

Lila grinned. "There's no speaking involved, and if you're worried about looking stiff, I could coach you."

He didn't respond but turned off the highway onto a gravel road. She'd forgotten what a short ride it was between town and their camp. Out here among the bare trees, pines and thick underbrush, it seemed they were miles away from civilization. They'd been lucky to find a clearing large enough to accommodate the trailers and temporary corrals.

"Where to?" Clint asked, slowing the truck to a crawl to avoid crew members walking around in their own little worlds.

"Past the catering truck and generators." Lila pointed

to the row of trailers. "The second one. Home sweet home. God, I'm sick of that tin box."

"Is that where you work or…?"

"It's where I sleep and keep my clothes and stuff. And what's even better? I share it with two other women, one of whom happens to be a total slob."

"Why would you stay there—is the motel full?"

Lila laughed. "No. The Boarding House Inn and the motel are reserved for the director and cast, the screen-writer, what we commonly refer to as above-the-line personnel. We peons get to live like we're still in college."

"And you've been on the road for how long?"

"Three months." That it seemed more like a year probably had more to do with her recent lack of enthusiasm. "Oh, and Baxter gets to stay at the motel, but his uncle pays for that. It doesn't come out of our budget."

"Should I park?" Clint asked, sounding uncertain. "Or am I just letting you off?"

Lila glanced at the dark trailer. "My roomies aren't here. No telling what it looks like inside, but if you don't mind risking exposure to nuclear waste, you're welcome to come in."

He stopped the truck. "Okay if I park here?"

Lila chuckled. "Sure."

The slight jitter in her tummy was ridiculous. Nothing was going to happen in the stupid trailer, she thought as she climbed out of the truck. She could be called to the set at any time. Or Shannon or Diane could show up.

Lila jumped out and hurried to the door. If the place was beyond disgusting, she'd discourage Clint from coming in. "So, have I completely ruined your perception of Hollywood and all its glamour?" she asked over her shoulder.

"To be honest, I hadn't given it much thought one way or another."

Of course he hadn't. The world didn't revolve around Hollywood. Something most people in the business often forgot, including herself.

She pushed the creaky door open. It wasn't horrible inside; she'd seen it in worse condition.

"I guess I am surprised that making a movie doesn't take more people." He stopped on the first step and shook the rickety railing. "This is dangerous. It needs to be tightened," he said. "I have tools in my truck."

Lila stood just inside the door, staring at him. She couldn't quite find her voice, or breathe for that matter. It was such a kind, unexpected offer. A small gesture, and yet not really small at all considering he didn't know her.

He looked up, met her eyes and smiled.

"That's nice—but it's only three steps. No one uses the railing."

"Wouldn't take me long." He pushed up the brim of his hat, the warmth in his eyes turning them a golden brown. "And I'd feel better."

She held in a sigh. "As much as I appreciate it, my roommates could show up at any moment…"

Clint nodded. "Okay."

Lila turned and grabbed a pillow off the floor, then kicked Shannon's boots out of the way. Great. Diane had left her vibrator out. Lila dropped the pillow on it and spun to face Clint.

"So…" She shrugged. "Don't say I didn't warn you."

He eyed the two unmade beds heaped with a mix of dirty and clean clothes. Tubes of mascara, pencil liners and palettes of eye shadow and nail polish in every possible color were scattered among dirty dishes.

Oh, dear God.

Lila spotted a second vibrator too late. Really, Diane? Two of them? The hot pink one was a doozy, too. Very fancy and clearly meant to leave no nook or cranny untouched.

Huh. Weirdly interesting. Lila would have to get a better look at it later.

Of course Clint spotted it right off. He frowned, angling his head to the side, as if he was trying to figure out how it worked.

"It's not mine," Lila blurted and felt her cheeks burn.

"Okay." Clint gave a slow nod. "That's what I thought it was," he muttered, ending with a short laugh.

The place really was a disaster, and yet a minute ago Lila had decided it wasn't so awful. When had she grown accustomed to living in a pig sty? When had her standards fallen so low?

"That's my bed back there," she said, jerking a thumb over her shoulder. "I make it every morning."

He gave her a sympathetic smile, and she buried her face in her hands.

"I'm sorry. I shouldn't have let you come in here," she moaned, her voice muffled.

"Hey, it's okay. I'm not all that neat myself." He put his hands on her shoulders and squeezed lightly. "And I have two brothers, remember? Everything was always a mess at the house. You can talk to my mom. She'll confirm it."

Lila smiled a little, even though he'd just lied. His truck was spotless. She uncovered her face, but she kept her chin lowered and her gaze on his chest. "This movie is important. We've got a real chance to get a deal with a distributor and after having begged, borrowed and bartered, we're still operating on fumes. That's why we have limited crew. Those of us who've invested in the project are working twice as hard, doubling up and overlapping jobs. Doing anything and everything to make sure the film succeeds. I've put in every last penny I'd saved and then some. Erin did, too. This has been our dream since we were in the third grade."

He kept massaging her shoulders and whispering that everything would be okay in that low velvety tone that was beginning to hypnotize her into believing him.

"I'm not complaining."

"I didn't think you were."

"Oh, Lord. Why am I even telling you all this? You're a stranger."

"Sometimes it's easier," Clint said, and rubbed a knot in back of her left shoulder.

"Well, fine, feel free to unload. Whatever you want to get off your chest, go for it."

"If I think of something, I will."

"Oh, so your life is perfect? That makes me feel so much better."

He laughed, the sound a low quiet rumble that wrapped her in his warmth. "It's not perfect," he said. "More like...predictable."

Lila couldn't tell if he thought that was good or bad. She lifted her chin and was rewarded with a smile that reached his eyes. "Want to hear something really sad?"

"What's that?"

"As horrifying as this pit is, I don't care half as much as I do about not having a tub. We have a shower. A tiny stupid shower. I would kill for a tub. Any plain generic one would do."

"I'm surprised you're not sharing a trailer with Erin."

"Ah." Lila nodded. "Normally we would have. But she met someone. He lives here, actually. Spencer Hunt.

He owns Moonlight Mountain. So she's been staying with him at his ranch."

Clint's hands stilled and his brows rose. He looked shocked, confused, curious. All appropriate reactions, but only for someone who knew Erin. Lila had no idea what was going through Clint's head.

"Do you know Spencer?" she asked.

"No. I've heard of him, though. He's been volunteering at a local animal sanctuary."

"They've invited me to stay with them," she said. "But Shadow Creek is too far."

"What is it, about thirty minutes?"

"I don't have my own car, and I never know when I'm needed on the set." She skipped the part about feeling like a third wheel. And the odd feeling she'd been having just recently that something was bothering Erin. Lila hoped it had nothing to do with Spencer. But, she was sure Erin would fill her in soon. "Anyway, predictable doesn't describe my life, that's for sure."

"You have anything pressing to do right now?" His eyes were beginning to darken, a clear hint that he had something in mind for her, something she was going to like.

"Nothing at all."

He put his hands on her waist and pulled her toward him. "How badly do you think Baxter needs me to agree?"

Unprepared for the switch in gears, she laughed. "I'd say he's pretty desperate if he asked me to help. I know he's zero for three with Jason."

Clint wrapped his arms around her. "Tell Baxter to put you up in the motel in town, and I'll do whatever he wants."

Lila stared at him. "Huh?"

"With his own money." Clint paused. "Or his uncle's, I don't care which."

"But—I—" She laughed. "I can't do that."

"Why not?" He brushed a kiss across her mouth. "Would you rather I call him?"

"No." She couldn't think. Not when her body was flush against his and she could feel him getting hard. "I don't know."

"Whatever you want, Lila," he whispered, his lips searing a path to her throat.

She swayed in his arms. His strong, muscled arms. How weird was it that she didn't feel nervous with Clint? She'd never kissed a man five minutes after meeting him. Okay, it had been longer but not all that much. She was always careful about not playing into the Hollywood stereotype. She didn't play fast or loose. Actually, it just wasn't her style.

She felt the tip of his tongue trace her collarbone. Her nipples tightened. She squeezed her thighs together. Her breathing was off, and she couldn't seem to drag in enough air.

"Tell me what you want, Lila." His voice was low and rough, his breath hot on her skin.

Her sweatshirt was too thick. She couldn't feel him pressed against her the way she wanted to...

He stopped kissing her and lifted his head. The second he stepped back, she heard the laughter just outside the trailer. She recognized Shannon's loud snort.

Lila stepped back, as well.

"So, you can tell him," Clint said when they heard the doorknob turn, "or you can give Baxter my number. That's up to you." He turned and nodded causally at Shannon and Diane as they entered, both of them speechless, eyes full of curiosity.

"I have to think about it," Lila said, her voice hardly shaking at all. But she almost lost it when he took off his hat and held it in front of himself. "I'll need your number."

Her cell signaled a text. They needed her on the set.

Clint surprised her with a business card. "I should probably get your number, too."

5

THE NEXT MORNING Clint dclegated the few chores he normally handled to Heath, the new man they'd hired last month. Then Clint left a note for his dad, letting him know he was taking some time off, and another note for the other three men who worked for them. He hadn't mentioned where he was headed, just that he'd be gone all day.

They'd all razz him if they knew he'd be standing around like some jackass while someone shot film of him. It wasn't as if he could keep it a secret. Eventually word would spread. He just didn't want anyone showing up to watch—or asking him why he was charging out of the house in his good clothes.

He filled a to-go mug in the kitchen and made it to his truck without anyone seeing him. But he managed to spill coffee on the new jeans he'd just put a crease in and cussed up a storm, trying to figure out what he should do about it. He decided the spot would be fine once it dried. And anyway, he didn't have time to change.

He reversed out of the garage and drove all of ten feet when he saw his dad coming from the stable. Clint considered pretending he hadn't seen him…then his dad motioned for him to stop.

Damn.

Clint let down his window. "Hey, Dad. What were you doing in the stable this early?"

"Just checking on Hazel. I thought she might be favoring her hind leg," he said, frowning as he got closer. "That a new shirt?"

"I left you a note. In the kitchen. So, how's Hazel?"

His dad chuckled, looking younger than he had in a long while. Now that he'd filled out some, his clothes were starting to fit him again, and his coloring was better. Years of stressing over finances had aged his father.

"I think she's okay. I'm not gonna call Doc Yardley yet." He paused, obviously waiting for Clint to say something. Then he smiled. "It's okay, son. You're a grown man. No need to tell me where you're going. It's none of my business."

Clint laughed. "I might've believed you if you weren't staring me down like I was sixteen again."

"I won't deny you got me curious."

"Dad, if a man puts on a new shirt and it's not Sunday—"

"It's a woman."

"That's right." Clint gave him a nod. "And that's all I'm saying about it."

"Your mom's going to be real happy."

"Only if someone opens his big mouth," Clint said and powered the window up, cutting off the howl of laughter that had him chuckling along with his dad.

He drove slowly down the gravel driveway, glancing in the rearview mirror and watching his dad dab at his eyes. How long had it been since he'd laughed like that? Too damn long. It was a great thing to hear. Despite the guilt tightening like a fist in Clint's chest.

For four decades Doug Landers had struggled with the responsibility of running Whispering Pines, choking from fear of failure and nearly destroying the legacy entrusted to him. What he knew about raising cattle, which was a hell of a lot, was equaled by how little he knew about business. But now that he saw an end in sight, he could finally breathe.

And Clint was that end.

It didn't seem to matter that he'd taken over the books years ago. And that he'd been the one going to auctions, deciding when to send the cattle to market and handling the daily operation of the ranch. Something about his dad knowing he'd soon officially hand over the reins had given him a new lease on life.

Dammit, how could Clint make any other decision but to take over?

He'd made it halfway to town before his brain finally settled. Thinking about Lila and knowing he'd be seeing her soon calmed him down some.

That she'd called soon after he'd left her last night had given him hope. Hope for what exactly, he wasn't sure. Sex would be a good start.

Damn, but he liked her. For so many more reasons than he could've guessed, considering she was beautiful and lived in a sophisticated world that was foreign to him.

After he parked in the same spot as yesterday, he checked the visor mirror to make sure he didn't have shaving cream on his face. He dragged a hand across his jaw. Smooth as a baby's behind. Hadn't missed a single spot.

Most of the people milling about were movie folks.

He didn't see Lila, though he was early. Catching sight of Baxter, Clint wondered what exactly she'd told him. By the time he'd gotten her voice mail and returned her call she was busy working, and they had all of twenty seconds to talk.

Clint decided to stay put for now. Wait until he got the chance to talk to Lila. He was dead serious about the motel being the thing that sealed the deal. Other than getting to see her, he wasn't looking forward to this bullshit. He would have rather paid for her to stay somewhere nicer, but he knew she wouldn't have accepted the offer.

He still hadn't made sense of her involvement with the film and why she'd invested her own money. She'd really confused him.

Thinking he saw her walking with Erin near the corrals, he straightened. Yep, it was her. His heart kicked into high gear. He paused long enough for a final inspection of his good boots, then he got out of the truck.

Lila spotted him right away. She waved, said something to Erin and the two of them veered toward him. He started walking to meet up with them, enjoying the snug fit of Lila's jeans and the curve-hugging sweater that showed off a lot more than yesterday's sweatshirt.

A good four yards away, Lila stopped and gaped at him.

"Something wrong?" he asked, and did a quick fly-check.

"What happened?"

Erin was shaking her head, not bothering to hide her amusement.

Clint loosened his collar. Damn shirt was a little stiff. "What do you mean?"

Lila advanced slowly. "You're not supposed to look

like this," she said, eyeing his jeans, his boots before glancing up and sighing. "You shaved. Why would you do that?"

Yes, Erin was *her* friend, but Clint looked to her for help, anyway.

Erin smiled. "Yesterday you wore faded jeans, scuffed boots. I don't remember the shirt—"

"Yeah, I was working." He swung a gaze at Lila. She was still frowning.

"Anyway," Erin continued. "That rugged, unshaven, hard-riding cowboy look you had going on? That's what Jason wanted."

Clint didn't know what to say. He rubbed his smooth jaw. "Baxter didn't say anything."

"I'm sorry," Lila said. "It's my fault."

"So…" Clint noticed people were staring. Yeah, just what he wanted—to be the center of attention. All because he'd cleaned up? There was something wrong with these people.

"Don't worry. Lila can fix you right up." Erin glanced at her friend. "Jason doesn't need him for another hour."

"He'll be ready," Lila said, checking her watch.

"Either Baxter or I will come get you," Erin told him. She turned to leave but glanced back with a grin. "Oh, and nice move getting Lila set up at the motel."

Clint wished she'd kept her voice down. A couple of complete strangers strolling by grinned and gave him a thumbs-up.

"Come on," Lila said, "and don't worry about the crew knowing. Everyone would've heard even if Erin and I hadn't spread it around." She tugged on his arm, trying to get him to move.

"Why would you let it get out?"

"Once the crew found out, which was inevitable, I

couldn't let them think Wild Coyote—our production company—was footing the bill."

"Explain something to me," he said as he walked alongside her. "You mentioned you'd invested money but you're working as a hairstylist instead of acting. Why?"

"I think I also said we don't have a big studio behind us. Erin and I met Jason and two of his friends, David and Brian, in film school. We hung out together, worked on projects together and really clicked. None of us had any connections in the business, so after school we looked out for each other—" Lila shaded her eyes from the sun and squinted at something. "Excuse me for just a sec."

She flagged down a young woman with short blue hair carrying a clipboard and then walked briskly to meet up with her. Lila's worn jeans really showed off her long slim legs, and her hair, tousled by the breeze, glinted gold in the sunlight.

Granted, he knew less than nothing about the entertainment business, but it was mind-boggling that a woman like her wasn't doing something more than grunt work behind the scenes. She wasn't just gorgeous, she seemed smart, level-headed, dedicated. The fact that he'd showed up at all, had agreed to act like a fool—and come to think of it, he didn't remember her even asking him to do it. He'd volunteered. Yes, the woman had a gift.

After she confirmed the hair-and-makeup trailer was available, they resumed walking.

"You were telling me about how you and your school buddies got to this point," he reminded her.

"Oh, right. About a year ago we realized none of us were getting anywhere and knew we had to make something happen. So we formed Wild Coyote Productions. Westerns have been in need of a revival, so that's where we're focusing our efforts. Lucky for Jason—for all of us actually—he inherited a nice chunk of money he was willing to sink into the project. That's why he's directing and not Erin. But this is still her best shot. She'll be first AD—that is, assistant director—for the sequel. David's a writer, so he and a friend collaborated on the script. Brian, Erin and I made the smallest financial contribution, but we've been working our tails off and paying ourselves just enough money to cover our expenses."

When they arrived at the trailer, Lila opened the door and peeked inside. "We have the place for thirty minutes, but it won't take that long." She turned and regarded him with a critical eye. "I don't suppose you have an old shirt in your truck."

"A T-shirt. Maybe. And an old denim jacket that I should've tossed in the rag bin."

"Oh, good." She gave him a smile that could turn winter into spring. "We'll get it later."

He followed her inside the trailer, mulling over what she'd just told him. It still wasn't clear what she'd end up getting in return for her investment.

"Go ahead and have a seat," she said, gesturing at a row of stools, and then crouched to rifle through a set of plastic drawers.

The stools were adjusted to different heights and faced a wall made up of mirrors. It resembled the beauty shop where his mom got her hair done once a month. He took a sniff. Kind of smelled like it, too.

He glanced around. More mirrors. Lots of them, on the opposite wall, some floor length, and there was even a mobile unit stashed in the corner. A few round hand-held mirrors and blow-dryers hung from nearby hooks.

"Finding anything interesting?" Lila asked, an amused lilt to her voice.

"Hollywood people sure like looking at themselves." He turned, and, momentarily blinded by a glaring white light, ducked his head. "And they want a lot of light while they do."

Lila grinned. "You're wrong. They'd prefer next to no light and that high-def be banned forever."

Yep, there were a lot of light fixtures. They just weren't turned on. The sheer number of tubes, jars and various other *stuff* lying around astounded him. Yet somehow everything seemed orderly.

"Ah." Clint didn't know what triggered it, but he finally figured out what Lila had to gain from her investment. Oddly, if he was right, he couldn't say the notion pleased him. "Will you be starring in the sequel?"

Lila looked at him and laughed. "Starring? Try supporting actress."

"Why?"

"Because no one knows who I am. We need actors the public likes or at least has heard of. Obviously they aren't big names because we couldn't afford them." She rose to her feet, gracefully, just like she did everything else. "Penelope Lane, for instance. You've heard of her, right?"

"Nope."

Lila frowned at him. "Really?"

"Really."

She turned away and flipped through a folder. "Here," she said, showing him a picture of a twenty-something blonde. "Now do you recognize her?"

"Sorry."

"Do you go to the movies at all?"

"Not much." He hated that she was staring at him like he was a dumb hayseed. No, that was unfair. She just looked surprised.

"Should I ask which movie you saw last?"

"Probably not."

Grinning, she squeezed his arm. "It's nice to know someone whose life doesn't revolve around Hollywood." She didn't move her hand, the heat from her palm seeping through the cotton shirt. "By the way, thank you."

"Just make sure Baxter holds up his end."

"I meant for fixing the railing after I left."

"Oh. Yeah." For some reason, her mentioning it embarrassed him. "It was nothing."

"And for doing this. What a kind and generous thing." She started rubbing his forearm with her thumb, then glanced at her hand and pulled away. "I should be ashamed of myself for letting you make that deal with Baxter."

"No, you shouldn't. Not when I did it for my own selfish reason."

Lila blinked at him, looking puzzled at first. And then her eyes filled with dread, as if she expected him to say something she didn't want to hear.

"Do you have any idea how much pleasure it gives me to do this? And not just because Baxter's an ass." Clint winced. "Um, it slipped."

A smile brightened her face. "Couldn't have said it better myself."

He liked the rosy flush that colored her cheeks and how her eyes sparkled. That same image of her from last night had replayed in his head and kept him up for hours.

"Darn it, Lila, I want to kiss you so bad."

"What's stopping you?"

"I didn't want you to think that I expected—" He faltered when she started to laugh. "Expected anything."

"Sorry," she murmured and pressed her lips together. "Me too. I wanted to kiss you, but I didn't want to give you the impression I felt obligated."

"Well, aren't we a pair," he said, and caught her by the waist, drawing her closer.

"Do I have to lock the door?" she asked, with an impish smile as she came up against his chest.

"You might."

"I'm supposed to be working."

"We'll get to that."

"Yes, but—"

Her lips were soft and warm. He felt the fast, steady thumping of her heart against his chest, echoing the rhythm of his own. She slid her arms around his neck as he skimmed a hand down her back. Lila was slender, but she still had enough curves to keep a man's hands itching for more.

She pushed her fingers into his hair, and when he cupped her bottom, she moaned into his mouth. He angled his head and kissed her deeply. Her tongue stroked his, fueling the need that had been burning inside him since last night. Lila moved her hips against him, and he knew there wasn't a chance she could've missed his erection.

It wasn't easy juggling good sense and desire. Maybe they *should* lock the door.

Clint thought he heard someone just outside. When Lila stiffened, he knew it hadn't been his imagination.

"To be continued," she whispered, and stepped back.

"Yes, ma'am."

His grin vanished when Baxter opened the door.

6

"WHAT'S THE HOLD UP?" Baxter looked directly at Lila and completely ignored Clint.

She figured that was probably fine with him. He was busy moving the only mobile stool around, either to give himself leg room or buying time for his erection to settle down.

The thought had her biting back a smile.

Lila cleared her throat. "What do you mean?" she asked Baxter. Echoing his deliberate rudeness, she focused on setting out her supplies without as much as a glance in his direction. "You can't be referring to Clint. Jason isn't ready for him."

Baxter responded with sulky silence.

Lila hoped it lasted for a while.

Clint finally abandoned the stool. "How's it going?" He slapped Baxter on the back and sent him stumbling forward. "I trust everything's been taken care of with the motel."

Baxter righted himself and adjusted his Ralph Lauren shirt collar. "Yes," he said. "And I prefer that our deal stays between us."

Clint glanced at her. "It makes no difference to me, but I don't see this thing staying quiet."

"Sit, please," she told Clint and shook out a plastic cape, forcing Baxter to move back. "Almost everyone knows."

"Already? Jason, too?"

"No. Not Jason," she said. "But eventually he'll find out."

"Who opened their big mouth?" With malice in his beady eyes, he glared at Clint.

"Erin and I put the word out."

Baxter turned and stared at her as if she'd betrayed him in some deep, profound way.

"What do you think the crew would say if they thought my room was coming out of the budget after asking everyone to sacrifice so much?" she asked. "You'd have a mutiny on your hands."

"I'm more concerned about what Jason will think," Baxter muttered.

"You got the job done. He doesn't care how you did it." She was about to fasten the cape around Clint's neck but changed her mind. "Would you mind horribly taking off your shirt?"

"Why?" Baxter's voice shot up two octaves.

"I was talking to Clint." She gave Baxter a wry look. "You can keep your shirt on. Please."

Chuckling, Clint started unbuttoning. She honestly hoped Baxter didn't faint. Lila wanted to get rid of him, not necessarily embarrass him. He did fine in that department all by himself.

Seeing the two men side by side, she couldn't help but feel some sympathy for Baxter. Clint was a good six inches taller, infinitely broader across the shoulders, and had nicely muscled arms and narrow hips.

To be fair, Clint wasn't an average-looking guy. But honestly, the two men didn't look as if they belonged to the same species.

He shrugged out of the shirt and she held her breath, hoping she wouldn't blurt out something stupid like, *can I lick your chest*? It was perfect. Just the right amount of muscle, just the right amount of hair scattered between his flat dark nipples. And not an ounce of spare flesh on his stomach. The hint of a six-pack was there but not *too* obvious, exactly how she liked it.

She cleared her throat and pretended she was auditioning for the role of Mother Teresa. "Let me hang your shirt so it won't get messed up," she said, modulating her voice. The sainted woman would not ogle or stammer over Clint's chest.

Clint passed her his shirt, and while she took it to the back of the trailer, she used the time to breathe deep and even. Deep and even. Deep and even. The brief calming exercise did the trick.

"You can go," she told Baxter. "Erin is coming to get Clint when it's time." She settled the cape over Clint and then fastened it at his nape. If Baxter hadn't been standing there, she might've been tempted to take a little nip. He smelled yummy.

"You're using the cape," Baxter said, sounding irritable. "Why did he have to take his shirt off?"

"Oh." She shrugged. "I just wanted to see his chest."

Clint choked out a laugh.

Baxter's pasty face turned red.

Lila was having a heck of a time controlling her own blush. Pulling off that line was harder than she'd guessed. At least she wasn't facing Clint. She leaned close to his ear and said loud enough for Baxter to hear, "Very nice, by the way."

Without a word Baxter headed for the door, but then paused with his hand on the knob. "Let me know when you're ready to check in, and I'll take you to the motel."

"I have a ride. Thanks, anyway."

Anger pinched Baxter's features. From the beginning he'd behaved like a petulant child used to having his way. And when he didn't get it, he pouted. But this was different. His hateful expression gave Lila a chill.

"Let me know if you change your mind." Casting a scornful glance at Clint, Baxter opened the door. "By the way," he said, his mocking smile aimed at Lila. "I had them put you in the room next to mine."

She held her breath until he was gone. "That's not going to happen," she muttered. "I'd rather stay in the trailer."

Her hand shook slightly. Grateful Clint couldn't see her, she pretended to fuss with the cape's Velcro fastener using the few seconds to calm down.

As she came around to face him, she saw he'd been watching her in the mirror. "I know what you're thinking," she said, busying herself with selecting the right brush. "I shouldn't have goaded him."

"Not what I was thinking."

"I'm not saying this is an excuse, but I wouldn't be giving him such a hard time if he hadn't come in throwing his weight around. He knows nothing about the business and is supposed to be learning. Instead, he makes everyone's job harder."

"I got the impression it's more personal with you."

She hesitated, not wanting Clint involved in any way. "He's asked me out a few times. Obviously I said no. But he won't leave it alone." She tried for a joke. "I figure annoying him is better than strangling him. Less red tape."

"Have you reported him?"

"Of course not. I can handle it." Right, Lila thought wryly. Because she'd done so well to that end. "I'm sorry I asked you to take off your shirt. It was unnecessary."

"I don't care about that." Clint looked serious. "How much do you know about Baxter?"

"Oh, he's harmless. I didn't mean to make a big deal of him asking me out. Lots of guys do. I ignore them." She realized how easy that was to misinterpret. "I'm impressing you left and right, aren't I?"

He cracked a small smile. "You're just stating the facts."

Lila sighed and nudged his chin higher so she could decide how dark she wanted to make the stubble. She touched the side of his face. His jaw was as smooth as could be. "I assume you shaved this morning and not last night."

"Afraid so."

"How much of a shadow will you have by late afternoon?"

"If I were going someplace that mattered, I'd have to shave again."

"Okay. That's good." She touched the other side of his face, his skin warm under her fingers. Her body welcomed the heat radiating from him, and she felt her breathing change. Uneven. Shallow. She didn't dare look into his eyes.

Except she did. And now she couldn't pull her gaze away from the dark seductive want mesmerizing her.

"How likely is it someone will be coming through that door?" His voice was low and rough.

"When?"

"In the next two minutes."

All she did was smile. Without waiting for an answer, he caught her wrist and kissed her palm. In the next second he'd pulled her onto his lap.

Surprised, Lila gasped but didn't resist. "I'll never have you ready in time."

"One kiss," he said. "That's all."

"Just one, huh?"

"Or two," he said, with a slow smile. "Your call."

She touched her lips to his but realized she was at an awkward angle. Shifting, she broke contact trying to find a better position.

He frowned at her. "Not like *that*."

"Hold on," she said, laughing. "I'm just getting more comfortable."

"No." He bit the side of her neck. "Forget comfortable. I want you on edge," he murmured against her skin. "Ready to explode."

Lila shivered. "Okay," she said weakly, closing her eyes as he trailed soft biting kisses to her ear.

Tilting her head to give him access, she put a hand on his chest. The plastic barrier frustrated her. She wanted to feel warm skin and soft hair beneath her palm. Maneuvering her hand under the cape would be impossible since she was sitting on the stupid thing.

He cupped her jaw, bringing her chin around until their eyes met. "I'll take that kiss now," he said.

Their lips touched. His arm tightened around her. The light pressure of his mouth increased, and she could feel him getting hard beneath her bottom. His tongue swept past her parted lips. She tasted coffee and the faint mint of toothpaste. His tongue stroked hers, and she eagerly met each caress with a stroke of her own. She felt weak, weightless, held together only by Clint's kiss and strong arms.

She wasn't at all prepared for his sudden retreat. Blinking at him, she tried to gather her wits. "What's wrong?"

"You didn't hear that?" He glanced at the door. "It's probably nothing," he said, releasing her, frustration in his eyes. "But we better not push it."

"No." She slid off his lap and had to clutch his shoulder to steady herself.

"You okay?" he asked, his hand going to her waist.

"Not sure," she murmured, surprised she was literally weak in the knees. No man had ever done that to her before.

She turned to pick up her stippling brush and dark eye shadow, and caught a glimpse of her flushed face in the mirror. Her eyes were bright, and her hair looked as if she'd just gotten out of bed. She quickly ran a hand through it.

The movement drew her attention to the other mirrors. She'd worked in this very trailer hundreds of times and had been totally clueless. You couldn't even blink without seeing yourself from three angles.

"Wow!" She swept a gaze all the way around, her pulse quickening. "This would be a pretty wild place to have sex."

Clint grinned. "Sweetheart, you read my mind."

THREE HOURS LATER, reminding himself he was doing this for Lila, Clint leaned against a cottonwood tree and stared off toward the foothills, trying his best to look *casually sinister*. Because if he had to do this take one more time, he was likely to use the gun stuck in the waistband of his jeans. It was just a prop, but he figured he could use the butt to beat Jason Littleton senseless. Clint wished someone had warned him the director was an asshole.

Casually sinister.

What the hell did that even mean?

"You're doing great," Erin said as she approached him. "We shouldn't be too much longer."

"Can I move? They aren't filming with you standing here, right?"

She nodded. "But don't get comfortable. You have only a couple minutes' reprieve."

"Your buddy, Jason—"

"I know. He's being a prick." Erin glanced over her shoulder. "Jason wasn't always like this. He's stressed over being so far behind schedule plus a bunch of other things. It doesn't excuse him..."

The director was early thirties. Tall, wiry, his blond hair pulled into a short ponytail. Clint knew Lila and Erin had gone to UCLA with him, and he could see the subject bothered Erin, so he let it drop.

"Lila wants you to know that when we break for lunch she'll meet you by the catering truck," Erin said, while studying the dark stuff on his jaw. "If that's okay with you."

"Yeah, sure." He felt chilly standing in the shade wearing a T-shirt and his thin, worn denim jacket. "Do you know how much longer they'll need me?"

"Most of the afternoon, I'm afraid. You're doing too good a job acting for them to let you go."

Clint shot Jason a look. He was still chewing out some poor kid holding a camera. "You mean, looking *casually sinister*?"

Erin followed his gaze and her smile looked more sardonic than amused. "Believe me, I get that you want to kill Jason. That's perfect. Keep thinking that, and we won't have to do many takes."

"I'll admit it," he said. "I was hoping the gun was loaded."

"If it was I would've beaten you to it." She clapped him on the shoulder. "Hang in there. This afternoon we'll be filming in town, so it'll be warmer."

His jaw nearly hit the ground. "Are you serious?"

"What's the problem? You didn't expect this to take so long, or you don't want your neighbors to see you?"

"Both."

She gave him a sympathetic nod. "Just remember it's for a good cause." A young woman yelled, "Places, everybody," and as Erin backed away she said, "Any chance you can take Lila to the motel this evening?"

"I'm planning on it," he said, despite not having asked Lila if that's what she wanted.

"Thanks." Erin turned and hurried toward a group of extras standing off to the side.

Clint recognized a couple of them. They were all young, looking eager and excited, and probably jealous that he'd been used in two scenes with close-up shots. Hell, he'd trade places with any of them in a hot second.

When he'd offered his services in exchange for Lila's motel room, he hadn't understood exactly what was expected of him. He would've minded a whole lot less if he was just a face in the crowd. Though he supposed it didn't matter. He'd liked seeing the way her eyes lit up at the idea of having a bathtub. He liked her, period. So yeah, he would've made the same decision either way.

Unfortunately, that didn't make the prospect of being on display for people he knew any easier. A few locals had been hired to build sets. Yesterday he'd seen them working at the edge of town. Even if they'd finished the job, wherever the crew filmed, they'd draw a crowd. He was just going to have to tough it out.

An hour later when they broke for lunch he had to remind himself of the greater good. Baxter shooting him looks that could kill didn't bother Clint. And he ignored Jason's occasional tantrums. Ironically it was Erin who made Clint want to rethink this whole movie gig as they left the set and went in search of Lila and food.

"Um, I hate to ask you this," Erin said. "But how would you feel about saying a few lines in tomorrow's scene?"

Clint snorted a laugh. "Hell, I think you already know."

She grinned. "Can I convince you to do it anyway? It pays more money."

"I don't care about that."

"Yeah, I figured."

The thing was, he liked Erin, but not enough to make an ass of himself.

After walking in silence for several minutes, Erin spotted Lila and flagged her down.

She changed course and headed toward them with a smile across her face, her hair loose and fluttering in the breeze.

"You know, Lila could take you somewhere private and help you learn your lines," Erin said.

He slanted her a look and caught her sly grin. "You wanna play dirty, huh?"

"Is it working?"

Clint turned back to Lila and sighed.

7

SHORTLY AFTER FOUR Lila had started straightening her work station. She was officially done for the day. But she knew it didn't mean Baxter or one of Jason's other flunkies wouldn't call and ask her to do something. For now, though, she wasn't arguing with Erin's directive. Not counting Jason, Erin was pretty much the boss around the set. Mostly because she was smart and very good at what she did, and that made her right 98 percent of the time.

Lately though, even Jason had been giving her a wide berth. Avoiding her when she was in a bad mood or deferring to her when it came to the crew. What troubled Lila was that Erin wasn't the moody type. Earlier Lila had flat out asked her if something was going on between her and Spencer, but according to Erin, all was fine with them. Still, something was off. Erin could be serious and focused, getting right to the point, but the detached attitude was new. And pretending everything was all right just made it worse.

She heard a brief knock before the door squeaked open.

Clint poked his head inside. "Erin told me to meet you here."

"Come in," she said, excited to see him, despite having eaten lunch with him only three hours ago. "Actually I'm finished, so we can leave."

"I'm totally down with that."

Lila grinned. "I see you still haven't caught the acting bug."

"Never gonna happen."

"I believe you." Grabbing her purse from a lower cabinet, she paused for a second. "Did Erin railroad you into helping me move?"

His mouth curved into a slow smile. "No."

"Are you sure?"

"Yes."

"You've been here all day. You must have a lot of work waiting for you at home."

"Even if that were true, do you think I'd leave you to Baxter's mercy?"

"I'm not helpless. I know how to tell him to get lost. Having said that…" She faked a shudder. "Thank you a thousand times over."

"My pleasure, ma'am," he said with a tug on the brim of his hat, looking sexy and adorable at the same time.

"I promise to pay you back, in full, with all the acting lessons you want."

His amusement vanished.

She paused. "Wow. You really don't want to…" Of course he didn't want to do that scene tomorrow. "Erin badgered you into it, didn't she?"

"Your friend should be a politician," he said, stepping back from the door and offering her a hand down the three steps.

Lila felt foolish accepting his assistance. After all, she'd run up and down them a million times all by herself. But when her fingers touched his callused palm, a tiny frisson of awareness blazed a path all the way down to her toes, and she just didn't give a flip how it looked.

"I assume we're going to your trailer to pick up your things," he said, to which she nodded. "You want to ride over with me, or would you prefer I meet you there?"

"Oh, I'm already packed. We can go together."

With a hand at the small of her back, Clint steered her in the right direction, and Lila set a quick pace, hoping to get out of there before someone called her to the set.

"You getting any grief over moving to the motel?" he asked once they were both in his truck.

"The crew thinks Baxter lost a bet. They're all very happy that I'm sticking it to him."

Clint smiled. "Where did they get that idea?"

"You know, Erin and I have been wondering the same thing."

"God help anyone who messes with the two of you."

"Darn straight." She saw his lips twitch. "You'd think after being in this business for six years I'd know how to swear. I mean, I can say the words, but not without turning ten unattractive shades of red."

"Cussing is overrated."

"It's supposed to be therapeutic. They have studies proving it's a stress reliever. Although, Erin can cuss with the best of them and I wouldn't describe her as very Zen."

"No," he agreed with a laugh. "She's more like a drill sergeant."

"Oh, she'd approve of that description." Lila smiled as he pulled the truck to a stop beside the trailer and shut off the engine. "Has Erin seemed snappy to you?"

"I'm not sure how to answer that. I'd say she's mostly all business."

"I'm sorry. That was a silly question. You don't even know her." She opened her door. "I'll only be a minute."

"I'll help with your bags."

She touched his arm when he turned to get out. "Diane might be napping. She works late tonight. I can handle my bags."

Clint nodded and stayed put. But when she emerged from the trailer a minute later, she wasn't at all surprised to see him standing just outside the door. Without a word he took both bags and deposited them on the small back seat.

"Anything else?"

"Nope. That's it."

"You travel light for a—" He cleared his throat and opened the passenger door. "How long is Baxter springing for the room?"

Lila grinned. "Travel light for a woman? Is that what you were going to say?"

"Me? Um…" He smiled. "Nope."

"Why, Clint Landers," she said, sliding onto the seat. "I bet you get away with all kinds of things with that sexy smile of yours."

His eyebrows shot up, and he looked somewhat embarrassed. "Sexy, huh? I'll take it," he said, his arm resting on the door as he bent forward. "Just don't mention it in public."

She leaned in for a kiss and realized she'd misread the move when she saw the surprise in his eyes. He responded by brushing his mouth across hers in a sweet, gentle kiss that demanded nothing more than a brief connection. Probably didn't want to embarrass her.

Clint straightened. "We'd better get going."

She noted the sudden flurry of activity around them. Anyone would've thought there had just been a shift change at a nearby factory. She couldn't explain it. If something unexpected had happened, it could mean she'd be getting a call soon and there went her evening.

After what had just happened, maybe it wouldn't be such a bad thing. Her mind kept returning to the perfunctory kiss. Had it been that long since she'd liked a guy? Had she completely forgotten how to behave around someone who mattered?

She waited until he'd started the engine before she murmured, "Sorry about before."

He reversed, and looked at her as he waited for people to clear the way. "For what?"

"I thought you were going to kiss me and I—I just misunderstood. I wasn't being pushy."

His silence made her wince inside. She turned away and watched Red and another stuntman wolf down hot dogs outside their trailer while they eyed Clint's truck.

"Lila," he said finally, "I always want to kiss you. I'm just not comfortable doing it in front of people you work with."

"Yeah," she said, unable to stop a smile. "That wouldn't be good. But it wouldn't be the end of the world, either."

A car came up behind them, and someone beeped the horn. Clint hit the accelerator but drove at a snail's pace until they were clear of all the slowpokes coming and going from their trailers.

"How many of you are part of the crew?" Clint asked once they were on the highway.

"About forty-five, I think. Indies usually have smaller crews." Lila rubbed her hands together and suppressed a squeal. "Oh, my God. I can hardly believe it."

"What?" Clint asked, glancing at her.

"I get to sleep in a real bed tonight. Soak in a tub

of warm sudsy water. Do you think each room has its own coffeepot?"

"I have no idea. The motel just opened a month ago."

"That's okay. The bed and tub are key…anything else would be a bonus."

They turned onto Main Street and passed the service station and the pawn shop.

"That inn there on the left," Clint said, indicating an older white building with a wide porch. "My sister-in-law owns it. Unfortunately the rooms only have showers."

"Too bad. It's a cute place."

The town had gone all out decorating for Christmas. The words *Season's Greetings*, lit in bright red cursive, arched over the street. Thousands of white lights were woven into green garland. Lila twisted around as they passed a sign for The Cut and Curl.

"Was that a hair salon?" she asked.

"I think it's probably more beauty parlor than salon."

"Ah. How many are there in town?"

"Just the one as far as I know."

"Huh." She noticed quite a few vehicles parked in front of the Watering Hole. Next to the bar was a bank with a beautiful Christmas wreath hanging on the door. "I bet some hairstylists work out of their homes."

"Is that what you used to do before you wanted to be an actress?"

"No, but in film school, pretty much everyone worked every job. Especially on student productions. I discovered I had some talent in that direction and I actually liked doing hair, so I picked up tips while doing different jobs on movies and commercials. Lots of wannabes work as restaurant servers or parking valets to pay the bills. At least doing hair has kept me involved in some aspect of the business while I—" She sighed. "Wait for my big break." God, that sounded so cliché.

Funny, it had never bothered her before. But for some reason, it felt like she should have found that break before she'd turned twenty-eight. Still, she hung on, clinging to her old dream with everything she had. Anyway, she'd worked too hard to get this far and give up.

At the other end of Main Street, the brand-new motel with its red roof and oversized welcome sign came into view. The big cheesy blowup Santa and snowman sitting on either side of the parking lot entrance was just what she needed.

Clint laughed along with her as they turned into the lot and pulled up to the three-story building.

"Well, it's not the Hilton." He stopped the truck. "Do you see a sign for the office?"

"No, but look at that." She pointed to the glass doors under an overhang. "They have a lobby."

"Hey, pretty snazzy."

"I'll say." She got her phone out and snapped a picture to send to her mom and sister. "Oh my, this is so exciting."

Clint stared as if he didn't know what to make of her. "How long have you been living in that trailer?"

"Too long, evidently." She felt her face heat, then she laughed and gestured to a vacant parking spot in front of a marked exit door.

He insisted on carrying both of her bags, so Lila took another picture before they entered the lobby. It wasn't much, just a small sitting area with a pair of burgundy club chairs, a brown loveseat and a few magazines on a small table. Lila's gaze went straight to the Christmas tree in the corner.

Standing over ten feet tall, it was decorated with blue

and gold ornaments and hundreds of blinking lights. The tree was real, not artificial, and she breathed in the sweet pine scent, releasing it when she felt a pang of homesickness.

She glanced at Clint. "I bet they found this tree locally."

"I'd put money on it. That's one thing we've got plenty of."

"May I help you folks?"

They turned to a dark-haired woman who was standing behind the reception desk.

"Well, for goodness' sake, Clint Landers, I didn't know that was you." She was medium height, maybe forty, with laugh lines fanning out from her blue eyes. "You need a haircut, mister."

Lila gasped. "Oh, no. Don't say that."

Clint grinned. "Hey, Patty, how you doing?"

The woman didn't answer. She was staring at Lila.

Probably thought Lila was the rudest person on earth for butting in like she had. "I only said that about his hair because—"

"Lila." Clint put down a bag and touched her lower back. "Let's get you checked in before Baxter shows up."

The warm steady feel of his hand pressed against her spine felt so much better than it should have. Exhaustion was really getting to her, that and the nostalgia of the holidays. Why else would she react so strongly to the touch of a man she barely knew?

"Lila Loveridge," Clint said, looking at her. "I assume that's how the reservation would've been made."

Lila snapped out of it and nodded.

"Is that your real name?" Patty asked.

"Yes." She smiled, not in the least surprised. It was a common question.

Patty blinked. "Heavens," she said, waving away her blush. "I'm acting like a starstruck teenager. Please pardon my manners. Just last week I scolded the day clerk for behaving like that when Penelope Lane and Dash Rockwell arrived."

"It's okay. I'm not a cast member. I'm part of the crew, the hairstylist, actually."

Patty frowned, then glanced at Clint.

He nodded, shrugged.

"Well, ain't that a shame," Patty muttered and went to work on her keyboard. "Yes, here you are. Your reservation was made by Mr. Mortimer, and you're staying for two weeks?"

Lila's unladylike shriek made Patty look up. Clint just laughed.

"Yes," she said demurely.

The second Patty returned her attention to the computer screen, Lila looked at Clint, held up two fingers and mouthed *two weeks*.

He was smiling, but faint worry lines had formed between his brows. "Mortimer? Is that Baxter Mortimer?"

"Oh, right." Lila turned to Patty. "Could you please make sure my room isn't anywhere near his?"

The woman hesitated. "Actually, he made a special request that you be put right next to him."

"That won't work." Lila bit her lip. She could see the poor woman wasn't sure how to handle the situation. But her name tag did indicate she was the night supervisor. "I know he's paying, but I'm the named guest. Shouldn't my request count more?"

She let out the most pitiful sigh.

"Look, Patty," Clint said, "if this puts you in a bind—"

"You know me, Clint. I'd be more than happy to oblige if I could. The manager handled the reservation personally. And truth be told, with my two older ones away at college, I need this job."

"I understand," Clint said, nodding. "Do I know the manager?"

Patty shook her head. "Kevin's a young fella out of Kalispell. He oversees a motel there along with this one. In fact, you just missed him."

"Maybe I could call him?" Lila knew it was a bad idea the second Patty's expression fell. "That's okay," she said. "If Baxter annoys me, I'll just go back to base camp. No problem."

"He won't bother you," Clint said in a quiet voice. "I'll take care of it."

Lila studied the strong set of his jaw, saw the confidence in his dark eyes and her heart beat double time.

"Granted, I don't know this Baxter fella," Patty said. "But I know Clint, and for what it's worth, my money's on him."

Lila bumped him with her shoulder. "Something about you I should know about?"

"Oh, honey, the stories I could—" Patty stopped abruptly after one look from Clint.

"We done here?" he said, and picked up the bag he'd set down.

"If I could just get you to sign this…" Patty slid the electronic signature machine toward Lila. "We serve coffee in the lobby all day. I was about to make a fresh pot if you're interested. And from seven to nine in the morning, we set out an assortment of muffins, doughnuts and cinnamon rolls, all made fresh right here in town."

Lila thanked her, accepted the room key and led

Clint to the elevator. Once they were inside the car, she pressed the button for the third floor. "Not too bright of Baxter," she muttered, annoyed with the man's gall. "I could do some serious damage shoving him off the balcony."

Amusement gleamed in Clint's eyes. "Something I should know about *you*?"

"Yes," she said, smiling up at him. "I like kissing. A lot." She slid her arms around his neck. "With you."

8

LILA FUMBLED TRYING to unlock the door. But as soon as she succeeded, her arms went right back around Clint's neck.

Managing not to lose her bags, Clint pushed the door open with his elbow and backed into the room with her clutching his shoulders. Her lips clung to his lips, and her breasts, her nice, round breasts found a home against his chest.

Damn, who knew 317 was his lucky number?

A few steps in and they cleared the door. He let it close and dropped both bags just as she pushed her fingers through his hair. She had one hell of a touch. He'd never had a spine-tingling reaction to a woman rubbing his scalp before.

He put his arms around her and held her tight, keeping his boots planted until he was sure they weren't about to take a tumble. Everything had happened so fast he didn't even know how close they were to the bed. Not that he was presuming anything. But a man could hope. And that *hope* was getting harder by the second.

No other woman had ever felt this good in his arms. Or tasted this sweet. She let out a breathy sigh as his tongue stroked hers, the intoxicating sound going straight to his cock. The sway of her hips, as if she were dancing to a song in her head, sorely tested his self-control.

He rubbed a hand down her back, stopping at the tempting curve of her bottom. He didn't want to stop. And he didn't think she'd tell him to, but for some crazy reason, he decided Lila was a woman he wanted to go slow with. He wanted to learn the contours of her mouth, see all her different smiles, make her eyes shine like they did when she was excited about something. Even something as simple as a motel Christmas tree.

It made no sense. His wanting to woo her slowly. She wouldn't be here long. Any time they spent together would be over in the blink of an eye. Lila was on the road to a bright future. She didn't have room in her life for a cowboy stuck running the family ranch.

The thought rattled him.

He'd never felt trapped by his family or the Whispering Pines, and he sure couldn't afford that line of thinking now. Not with the big decision he had to make.

Clint changed the slant of his mouth and kissed her more deeply. Her fingertips dug into his scalp with just the right amount of pressure. Her breasts pressed against the lower part of his chest, and he could feel her hardening nipples through the layers of their clothing. What he wouldn't give to see all of her, to feel the warm softness of her skin...

Her sweet, sexy moan almost undid him.

He broke the kiss. Slowly. As slowly as he could without dropping to his knees.

Lila gave a slight jerk when he moved his head back. He gently pried her arms from around his neck, and she blinked at him. "Sorry," she murmured. "I don't know what got into me."

Wishing it had been him, he held back a groan. Ordered his cock to be patient. Hoped like hell his brain still had control over his mouth.

He put it to the test with a smile first. Reasonably encouraged, he stepped back and said, "I was afraid you'd trip over your bags."

She frowned at the lame excuse.

"Look, Lila—"

She had a dark smudge on her left cheek. Or was it a shadow? He caught her chin, angling it so he could study the rest of her face.

"What are you doing?"

"You have something on your face." He rubbed his thumb over a second smear.

"Oh." She touched her cheek and grinned. "I know what that is. Come with me."

Following her, he noticed it wasn't a bad room. Done up in green-and-cream, it had a king-size bed, a table with two upholstered chairs, and a small dresser. The open drapes showed off a partial view of the Rockies in the distance.

Light flooded out of the bathroom.

He saw Lila standing in front of the sink. His gaze drifted back to the bed before he joined her.

Damn his one-track brain.

Washcloth in hand, she stared at herself in the mirror, dabbing at her nose. Even in the terrible artificial light, her skin was smooth and perfect. Before he knew what he was doing, he touched her cheek.

She turned her head and smiled at him. "Did I miss a spot?"

"I don't know." He laughed and lowered his hand. "Let's see." Of course he fixated on her lips, pink and damp from all the kissing.

"Okay, let's take care of you."

"Huh?" He met her eyes. Something crackled in the air around them. Did she mean...?

They just stared at each other for a long drawn out moment. Blood pumped hot and fast to his groin. She turned to rinse out the washcloth and then tugged him closer.

"I thought I'd gotten all of it," she said as she dabbed at his chin. "Your stubble is already coming in so it fooled me."

Clint finally understood what had happened. He took a quick look in the mirror but didn't see any of the goop she'd used earlier.

"There." She dropped the washcloth into the sink and cupped his chin. Mimicking his earlier move, she angled his face to the left, then to the right for her final inspection. "You're good to go."

"As in you want me to leave?"

"No." She shook her head, smiling. "Unless you want to." She let go of his chin and dried her hands on a towel. "I mean you did your good deed, and I'll be fine."

"Actually I was wondering if you were hungry."

She gave him a tentative look he couldn't read.

"I'd like to take you to dinner," he continued. "There's a new steak house down the street. I haven't been there yet. It opened only a couple months ago." He paused, leaving her time to say something, but she didn't. "I heard it's pretty good."

"I was pushy," she said, staring at her hands. "You know...before. I swear I'm not usually like that. I'm really not."

"Lila?"

"I'm just saying you can leave, and it won't hurt my feelings."

"Hey…"

She glanced up.

"I didn't think you were pushy. After our talk last night, I thought I had to wait until Saturday to take you out, so believe me when I say I'm as happy as a flea in a doghouse—" He stopped. Had he just sounded like his granddad? "I have no idea where that came from, so if we could just forget that bit of down-home whatever…"

Lila's laughter put the sparkle back in her eyes.

He found himself smiling back at her. And oddly, it seemed as natural as breathing for him to put his hands on her waist. "I'm going to make it real plain," he said. "You know what's going to happen between us if we stay here, don't you?"

Her smile wavered a bit. "I really like you, Clint," she said, and he knew what was coming next. "I don't think I'd mind if something did happen…"

Not what he'd expected. "You don't look all that sure," he said, "so how about we wait until you are?"

Her lips lifted in a soft smile that he brushed with a brief kiss.

He'd done the honorable thing, and it felt good. And at the same time so goddamn disappointing.

Go figure.

And now he had to take a giant step back before he screwed up everything by stealing the kind of kiss he really wanted.

LILA WOULDN'T HAVE minded walking the few blocks to the steak house if the air hadn't been so chilly. Clint found a parking spot in front of a bakery that Lila had missed earlier.

"The Cake Whisperer," she said, reading the sign as she slid out of the truck. "How cute. Looks new."

Clint nodded as he closed the passenger door. "The Full Moon Saloon opened sometime back in July. Then the bakery and steak house opened right after. Nice to see the town thriving, especially around this time of year. Speaking of which, don't you have a jacket with you?"

"Not so much for this temperature," she said, wrapping her arms around herself and trying not to shiver. Her black sweater was made of a decent weight cashmere blend, but she was foolish to have paired it with a short denim skirt in this weather.

She was sick of wearing jeans all the time, even though Clint assured her the steak house wasn't anything fancy and they would do fine. But mostly she'd wanted to look nice for him. Yeah, her chattering teeth were probably so attractive.

Looking out of place, the restaurant's flashing pink neon sign lorded over a row of early-bird specials handwritten with black marker and taped to the window. She didn't stop to have a look but hurried into the welcoming warmth of the dimly lit steak house. The heavenly smell of sizzling meat woke up her taste buds.

A middle-aged woman wearing a Frosty the Snowman sweatshirt came bustling from the back. "Evening, folks," she said, grabbing menus from a basket next to an old cash register. "Anywhere in particular you wanna sit?"

Clint glanced around. Only two tables were occupied; it was still early. "How about the corner booth? Should be fairly quiet back there."

The woman laughed. "Well, I hope it's not too quiet," she said over her shoulder as she led them to the booth. "We could use the business."

"Has it been slow?" Clint sounded surprised.

"Nah, not too bad considering it's so close to Christmas. Having them movie people in town helps a lot. A few of 'em eat here almost every night."

Lila bet she could name which ones and prayed they were held up on the set until she and Clint were gone.

"That's good," he said. "Good for the whole town I imagine."

Lila slid into the booth. The woman passed her a menu, narrowing her eyes as if she'd just seen Lila for the first time.

"You must be one of them," the woman said.

"Yes, I'm with the crew. And by the way, cute sweatshirt."

The woman glanced down. "Oh, my grandkids surprised me with it last year. I like it. Get a lot of compliments, too." The door opened, and she glanced in that direction. "You folks take your time looking over the menu. I'll be back in a jiff."

"See?" Clint said. "I don't know everyone in town."

"Just every woman under forty."

He snorted a laugh. "Now why would you say that?"

"Because you're hot," she said and laughed at his exaggerated eye roll. "If you slide a little closer, I promise not to maul you under the table."

"Sweetheart," he said in a low, gravelly voice as he leaned forward, "that's not what I'm worried about. So, I believe I'll stay right where I am."

"Really?" Lila pretended to pout. "I promise to slap your hands if you try anything."

Clint shook his head. "Just look at your menu."

She held in a laugh. "I already know what I want. A baked potato with butter, sour cream and anything else they can pile on it. And maybe a small rib eye.

Hey, wait." She frowned at the menu. "They must have dessert."

"On the back." The woman who seated them had just stopped at the table. "Shoulda told you right off my name's Irene. I can get your drinks while you're still having a look."

Lila asked for water with lemon, and Clint ordered a beer.

When more people entered the restaurant, another woman, younger, with reddish hair gathered in a ponytail, came from the kitchen to seat them.

Tempted to turn around, Lila kept her face averted. "If Jason or anyone you recognize from the set comes in, would you let me know?"

"Sure. So far it's been locals." He glanced around. "Is it a problem for you to be here with me?"

"No. Nothing like that. I'm really lucky to have this extra night off and I guess I just don't want to see anyone. Except Erin, of course." She smiled, despite the sharp pang brought on by thinking about her friend. God, she missed her so much. It wasn't just about sharing her with Spencer, although that was taking some getting used to.

"You asked me about her mood earlier," Clint said, studying her closely.

"Did I?"

"We don't have to talk about it."

Well, so much for her stellar performance. "It's just that Erin hasn't been herself lately. She's been too subdued."

"Subdued?" Clint laughed. "She must've been hell on wheels before."

"Yep. That's Erin." Lila waited until after the redhead had set down their drinks. "When it comes to the job, she gives 200 percent. She has more enthusiasm and energy than anyone I know. We've been friends forever, so we've been through a lot together. There's never been a taboo subject with us."

Irene returned with a pad and pencil. "Did I give you folks enough time to decide?"

"I'm ready," Clint said. "Lila?"

Her appetite had dwindled, but she ordered the potato and a small salad. So did Clint, along with a large cut of rib eye.

He studied her a moment. "Hey, how about we both slide in a little bit?"

Lila smiled. "Okay, but remember there's no tablecloth."

"Well, damn." He pretended to be surprised, leaning back and checking under the table. "I'll let you see my hands at all times," he said, shifting toward the center of the black vinyl seat and getting a grin out of Lila.

She'd already been sitting farther in, so sliding a few inches put her within reaching distance of his arm and leg. "Now what?"

"Well…" He paused briefly. "Now you're close enough to snitch bites of my steak."

"Ah. I hadn't thought of that," she said and burst out laughing.

People were probably staring, and she didn't care.

She noted the humor gleaming in his eyes, then looked at his large tanned hand resting on the table. She already knew his palm was rough, but his touch was gentle. And that his clever mouth could send her soaring all the way to the moon and back.

And Lord, he was patient, and considerate. She'd sensed his disappointment back at the motel, but he hadn't pushed even a tiny bit. It had been Clint who'd applied the brakes, almost as if he knew she'd been feeling fragile lately. Unsure about her career, unsure about what was troubling Erin. And worried that sinking everything into this film would turn into a colossal mistake.

She hadn't been intimate with a lot of guys, but the few she had hooked up with had never expressed concern about whether she'd been ready to take the next step. She wasn't stupid. Her looks had played a big part in their attraction to her. Except for Jason. He'd shown an interest back in college. At least he hadn't been a jerk when she'd told him it was friends or nothing.

Clint moved his hand to cover hers and gave her a reassuring squeeze. She looked into his pensive eyes and smiled. How had he known that was exactly what she needed?

"Here you go, folks." Irene placed a salad in front of Lila. "Italian on the side for you," she said, then set down Clint's, covered with blue cheese dressing. In the middle of the table she placed a linen-covered basket. "Your dinners should be up soon."

They thanked her, and as she walked to the next table over, Lila peeked under the yellow linen napkin. Smelling the golden yeast rolls brought back her appetite.

"You think they're homemade?" She sniffed and made a moaning sound that probably embarrassed Clint. "I bet they are." She knew she shouldn't… The potato she'd ordered was a huge splurge. What with her big role coming up…

"Go for it," he said, grinning.

She hesitated…until she saw the glass ramekin of pale whipped butter. Her willpower evaporated like the steam from the warm rolls.

Lila grabbed the largest one. "You're a bad influence," she said as she slathered it with butter. "All these carbs are going to kill me."

"You barely ate anything for lunch." He tipped the beer to his lips.

"Don't forget, we still have to work on your speaking part for tomorrow. You can't afford to have me conk out on you."

That wiped the humor from his face.

Lila swallowed a small piece of roll. "Although, since it's a love scene, it shouldn't be a problem. I'm guessing you'll do very well."

Clint stared back, looking shocked. "You're joking."

"I thought Erin told you."

He pointed his fork at her. "You're messing with me."

"Why would I do that?" Lila asked, eyes wide, the picture of innocence. She could be a very good actress when she wanted to be.

9

LILA WAS SHIVERING by the time they arrived at the motel. She'd recognized Baxter's car even before they turned into the parking lot. The red Beemer convertible occupied the same spot they'd vacated a couple hours ago. Just the idea of it annoyed her, which said a lot about her anxiety level lately.

"Don't tell me," Clint said, glancing at the car. "It's Baxter's."

"How did you know? The California plates?"

"It's December in Montana. How many idiots would leave the top down?"

Lila grinned. Feeling a slight pinch near her ear, she realized it had come from her jaw joint. It actually ached from smiling so much. After dinner when she'd asked if they could drive around and look at Christmas lights, he'd agreed without even a blink. Of course they hadn't been gone long. Other than a pair of residential side streets, the ranches were spread out. Christmas was obviously a big deal around Blackfoot Falls, which made Lila like the place even more.

Clint pulled into a parking spot near the door, and her pulse jumped. He could've simply dropped her off, so maybe he wanted to come to her room. Although he hadn't cut the engine, so it was hard to know for sure. Lila appreciated that he'd been chivalrous before, but now she knew exactly what she wanted.

"Do you want—"

"How will you get—"

They spoke at the same time.

Clint motioned for her to go first. And then his phone chirped.

"Go ahead," she said when he didn't bother looking at it.

"Later. It's my mom."

"Oh, did you miss your curfew?" Her teasing apparently missed the mark.

Staring at the phone, he sighed. "How many times have I showed her how to text?"

"I can get out if you want."

"No. I'll only be a minute," he muttered, then shut off the engine and answered. "What's up, Mom?" He listened for a moment, frowning. "No way. I brought up every single box you had marked." He paused, chuckling under his breath. "No, ma'am, I stacked them in the same corner I do every year. The basement's not that crowded."

Lila typed a text to Erin. Nothing important. She just didn't want to make Clint uncomfortable or have him think he had to rush.

Clint stretched his neck to the side. "Fine. I'll check when I get home," he said, then turned his head and lowered his voice. "Yes, I did. In town. I have to go." He dropped his phone on the console and scrubbed a hand over his face. "Sorry."

"Don't be." She sent her text and pocketed her phone. "I should've just gotten out."

"That would've made things worse. Believe me, there's no crisis. She thinks some Christmas ornaments are missing."

"Are you insane?"

"Maybe," he said. "Could you be more specific?"

"Definitely a crisis. How long has she been collecting the ornaments? I bet they were passed down from your grandparents. Probably even from your great-grandparents." Lila sighed. "Why are you looking at me like that?"

"You're serious."

"Well, of course I am! Those kinds of things are irreplaceable."

"Okay. I see your point. But I know damn good and well it's all there. The minute I get home—" He couldn't have looked more disgusted if he tried. "How are you getting to the set tomorrow? Can I give you a ride?"

"I think Erin is going to pick me up. Did I say something to upset you?"

"No, it's not you. It's...nothing."

"Okay." It sounded as if he might live with his parents and maybe he didn't want her to know. "What time do they want you on the set?"

"By eleven."

"Lucky you. I start at seven."

Clint snorted. "Hell, I'll have fed and watered the horses by then."

"Wow. That's right. You have a bunch of ranch things to do."

He found her hand and gave it a light squeeze. "Don't feel too sorry for me. We have some hired men to help with the *ranch things*."

"Okay, I should've said chores. Would that be more

accurate?" How crazy was it that just the feel of his callused palm could make her skin tingle?

"I like *ranch things*. I'm going to start using it."

Lila laughed. "You've never told me exactly what you do."

"I'm the foreman, so I handle the daily operation, ordering supplies, payroll, buying and selling cattle at auctions. When it's roundup time, I work right alongside the guys."

"Does your father do anything?" She groaned. "I didn't mean that the way it sounded. Honestly, that was so rude."

Clint chuckled. "Let's just say he's semiretired…" He looked as though he was about to say something else but changed his mind. Whatever it was, his mood seemed to take a dip.

Lila shifted restlessly. "Thank you for dinner," she said. "And for getting me an amazing room."

"Amazing, huh?" He smiled. "Hey, I didn't look. Does it have a tub?"

"Oh, yeah."

"Has to be pretty generic."

"I'm not complaining." She drew in a breath. "Maybe you'd like to try it out with me some time…"

The moon lit most of his face. Desire flared hot in his eyes. "No maybe about it."

Lila's mouth went dry. She knew she should say something. Clearly it would be up to her if and when they were to take the next step. But she couldn't seem to think straight or even make her mouth work, which at the moment was probably a blessing.

She hated the timing. She knew she was overly touchy about sex being used as a favor; hard to live and work in Hollywood and not be aware of it. Clint was different. Knowing with absolute certainty his generosity came without strings attached helped, but not enough. Not in this particular instance.

What had tripped her up was thanking him for dinner and the room. It was appropriate, even though she'd already thanked him, but saying it again and then jumping into bed with him? Too weird. She liked him too much to give him the wrong impression.

He'd been watching her, and when she met his eyes again, he gave her a patient smile.

"I love the name Whispering Pines," she said, feeling like the biggest wuss in the whole world.

He didn't release her hand, so he hadn't written her off as a lost cause. "It's okay. Not very manly, though," he said with a shrug and a self-deprecating laugh. "The ranch has been in the family for generations. I think it might've been my great-great grandmother who came up with the name."

"Is it very far?"

"Thirty minutes."

She waited, hoping he'd suggest taking her there some time. The invitation didn't come.

"Am I going to see you tomorrow?" he asked.

"I'll make a point of it." She curled her fingers around his hand and leaned slightly toward him.

Clint took it from there. Sliding a hand around the back of her neck, he drew her closer as he leaned over the console until their lips met. The pressure of his palm against her nape had an odd and intoxicating effect on her. She parted her lips, anxious to feel the warm stroke of his tongue, and he didn't disappoint.

She tasted his hunger as he explored her mouth, her need for him growing with breathless speed. Shifting her body so that she faced him, her hand landed high on his thigh. His muscles tensed underneath her touch, and his low, husky moan filled her mouth.

Her heart seemed to stop.

Oh, how she regretted not inviting him to her room. It was silly to be sitting out here. She'd fretted for nothing. She would make the suggestion…

He'd deepened the kiss and she could barely stay still, much less think. He sucked on her tongue, nibbled her bottom lip and teased the corners of her mouth. He tilted her chin up and changed the angle of his head, then traced his fingers along her jawline before plunging them into her hair.

The loud bang of a car door changed the tempo.

Clint didn't pull away, but he tamed the kiss and relaxed his hand. He took his time ending things, but it didn't blunt the sense of loss she felt the moment he broke away.

His mouth curved in a smile as he brushed the hair away from her eyes. And then his gaze drifted past her to something outside. Something that caused his expression to tighten, and she couldn't resist a backward glance.

Over two dozen cars crowded the small lot. But of course it had to be Baxter. Standing beside his Beemer and looking in their general direction. Between the moon and the motel's floodlights, the visibility was good if he knew where to look.

Exasperated, Lila groaned. "You think he can see us through these tinted windows?"

"I wouldn't have thought so. But he slammed the door for a reason."

She hadn't considered that, but of course. He hadn't just arrived, and he obviously wasn't in a hurry to leave. "Should we give him a show?"

Clint looked at her. "You really want to do that?"

Her inner child was all pumped to say *you betcha*. "I guess not," she muttered, sitting back against the seat. "Stupid jerk. He's probably pleased with himself for killing the mood."

Clint looked as though he was about to say something, but changed his mind. "I'll stay here in the truck until you get to your room and he leaves. I'll make sure he sees me. Hopefully he'll take off and not bother you tonight."

Lila tried to think fast. It was a good excuse to invite Clint upstairs. "Or you could come up with me."

"I could," he said with a slow nod as he searched her face. "If that's what you want."

Oh, God, she hated being put on the spot like this. Despite the fact that she'd started it. Usually she had no trouble dealing with men. No was an answer she knew well. But it was different with Clint. Darn him.

Tempted to run a hand down his fly and ask him what *he* wanted, she huffed a breath instead. "What's today? Wednesday?"

"Yep."

"Okay." She put her hand on the door handle. "I'll see you on the set, but I'm going to be busy all day tomorrow and then we're shooting a twilight scene." She lifted the handle. "Don't even think about weaseling out of Saturday night."

Clint let out a laugh. "Nope."

"Now, go find your mom's ornaments." She opened the door and slid out. "Thanks again for…everything."

By the time she closed the door, he'd climbed out and was coming around the hood.

"What's wrong?"

He pulled her into his arms and kissed her until there

was no air left. Not in her lungs, and maybe not even in the whole state of Montana. She dragged her mouth from his with a gasp.

"Good night, Lila," he whispered and let her go.

"Uh-huh," she murmured, making sure her legs weren't too wobbly before she turned and walked straight to the motel entrance, and right past Baxter without a single word.

AFTER BEING RECRUITED to do makeup on the principals some time around eleven the next morning, Lila had been bombarded with work the rest of the day. She'd skipped lunch, which wasn't unusual, but she hated that she'd gotten only a glimpse of Clint. She'd completely forgotten his scene was being shot in town.

Erin had been just as swamped. They'd met up once, briefly, but too many people had been around so they couldn't really talk. In the old days, Lila would've called her the minute she'd left Clint last night and talked for an hour, with Lila spilling everything down to the last detail.

Things were different now that Spencer was in the picture. Erin wouldn't have minded if Lila had called. If anything, Erin would be royally pissed if she knew the reason for Lila's hesitation.

Instead of their traditional postdate chat, Lila had looked at pictures of the family Christmas tree that Britney had sent to her phone. God, she hated not being there to shop and make Christmas cookies, do all the things she loved about the season.

Why did life have to throw so many curveballs at once? Being a grown-up and working in *glamorous* Hollywood had sounded like a lot more fun at thirteen.

At 4:30 p.m., Lila finally had a chance to breathe.

She'd splurged on a scrawny wreath she'd found at the small grocery store in town and had just hung it on the trailer door when Erin jogged toward her, an apple in each hand.

"You got a few?" she asked.

"Not really."

"Come anyway." Erin stopped and frowned at the wreath. "That's pretty sad."

"I know. Better than nothing."

Erin turned to study Lila. "You probably didn't have lunch," she said, handing her an apple and pulling a flattened protein bar out of her jeans pocket.

Lila wasn't interested in the bar, but she knew better than to refuse it. "Where are we going?"

"Nowhere. I just wanted a chance to talk. Walk fast—"

"And look busy. Got it."

Munching their apples, they headed in the opposite direction of the craft services table where most of the extras had gathered. Lila knew there was a good chance Clint had left. Or else he was still shooting in town, but she swept a glance around anyway.

"Do you like Clint?" Lila asked. "I do. I like him."

Erin gave her a long look and laughed. "Yeah, I know."

"What? He's really a nice guy."

"Why are you being defensive? I agree. I wanted to hear about what happened at the motel. Why do you think we're power walking in the friggin' cold?" Erin shivered and put her hood up. "Did you have sex with him?"

Lila laughed. This was the old Erin. Thank God. "He took me to that steak house in town for dinner.

Then we drove around, rehearsed his lines and looked at Christmas lights."

Erin chewed and swallowed a bite of apple. "But did you have sex?"

"No. We didn't."

"Why not?"

"I met the man two days ago. Have you ever known me to hook up with anyone that fast?" Lila slowed down and studied her friend. "What is going on with you?"

"No, you're right." Erin slowed as well. They'd passed the last trailer, and no one was within earshot. Lately, a chance for a quick chat didn't get better than this. "Clint's different—" She shrugged. "You know how you get a gut feeing about someone. I think he's a good guy," Erin said, "and it's been a while since you've hooked up with anyone, so I was hoping the two of you had clicked…"

"Are you feeling guilty because you're staying with Spencer? Because if you are, knock it off. I'm happy for you. Spencer seems great, and if you weren't making time for him, I'd have to kick your butt."

Erin grinned. "You could try."

"Wipe that smirk off your face. I've been pretty darn good about sticking up for myself and being assertive."

"Huh," Erin muttered with a thoughtful frown. "You really have. Well, at least Baxter's good for something."

"Practice?"

"Yep."

They both laughed.

"Okay, one more thing," Lila said as they started walking again. "In the interest of full disclosure, I'm very envious of you and Spencer. Not to be mistaken for jealousy. Just please don't think you have to push Clint and I together. I like him. I really do." Staring at the Rockies, she sighed. "Things were going well last night, and I know it's stupid, but part of me kept waiting for something to go wrong. Once sex entered the picture... Well, I didn't want what we had to end in disappointment because I misinterpreted the situation."

Erin nodded with understanding. She'd been there with Lila, through the tears and regret, when she'd discovered a guy she really liked had been more invested in sex with her than in her as a person.

"Of course there's always that risk," Erin said. "But I think Clint's the real deal. Hell, I don't know, maybe there's something about cowboys. They're a different breed. Spencer certainly is."

Lila smiled, wondering if Erin knew how her face lit up every time she mentioned his name. "Clint and I have a date Saturday night. I'm pretty sure it'll have a happy ending."

"Bring it home, sister," Erin said, holding up a hand.

Lila slapped a high five.

They lost their grins at the sound of Erin's name riding on the brisk wind, and turned toward the voice.

Baxter was standing near the clothes trailer.

"Jesus, he's got a cell phone and a walkie-talkie," Erin said, acknowledging him with a wave. "The dumb ass probably doesn't know how to use them."

Lila groaned inwardly when Erin started toward him. "Hey, have you got anything for me?" she asked casually as she fell into step with her. "You know, in the interest of full disclosure?"

Dread flickered in Erin's face before she looked away. She shrugged. "I don't think so," she said. "If he turns up missing, everyone would know it's me. Catch you later."

Lila's chest tightened with the grim certainty she

hadn't been wrong. Something was going on with Erin. Yet, after a twenty-year friendship and countless secrets that bonded them, she'd chosen not to share it with Lila.

Her spirits lifted when she spotted Clint. He was talking to a wrangler near the corrals. Lila didn't hesitate. She changed course and headed toward him, and the comfort she knew he'd give her.

10

CLINT LEFT THE house through the kitchen door and cursed under his breath when he saw Joe and Paxton. It was Saturday evening, for Christ's sake. By now they should've been halfway to Kalispell looking to raise hell. Yet there they were, hanging out with Murray, all three of them standing too close to Clint's truck for it to be a coincidence.

As far as he knew, Paxton and Murray were still feuding over last week's poker game. Evidently it hadn't stopped them from planning an ambush.

The old-timer was the first to spot him. Murray turned and spit on the ground beside him before giving Clint a toothless grin. "Well, now, don't you look purdy."

Joe swung his gaze around. "Hey, boss, are those new boots?"

Clint ignored them.

Paxton let out a whistle. "New shirt and new jeans, too," he said, sizing him up. "Hell, son, looks like you're getting all Hollywood on us."

"Might be he's courting someone special." Murray's

pale eyes took on a mischievous gleam. "Anything we should know about, Clinton?"

"You sound like a bunch of bored old ladies." He pushed past them and opened the driver's door, their laughter grating on his nerves.

Hell, he'd known all along word would spread that he was an *extra*. No one knew the circumstance that had prompted him to sign on. Though he supposed that didn't matter. He wondered if they'd heard about the speaking part he'd managed to bungle. What a damn disaster.

Squinting through the smoke from his cigarette, Joe said, "You gonna tell us where you're going, boss?"

If it weren't for Murray, who'd been working at the Whispering Pines since before Clint was born, he would've let his middle finger do his talking. "Look, I've told you before not to smoke near my truck. It stinks up the cab."

"See, I knew it." Murray nodded smugly. "He's aiming to impress a lady."

Clint gave the old guy a slick smile. "Next time I see Mrs. Chesterfield, I'll be sure to let her know how much you love her corn pudding."

Mention of the doting widow wiped the amusement off Murray's face. "That ain't funny, Clint. That crazy old woman won't never stop pestering me."

"That's right," Clint said and slid into the truck. Paxton started to say something, but Clint cut him off. "The two of you are fired."

Paxton and Joe laughed.

Jesus. First his mom had grilled him with the persistence of the county prosecutor. And then while he'd calculated next month's feed order and closed payroll, his dad kept giving him curious looks. What did a guy have to do to get some peace and privacy around here?

The only thing Clint had told his folks was that Lila was part of the movie crew working as the hair and makeup person. Nobody had to know she was an actress. He couldn't imagine what kind of uproar that would cause.

After all the bitter feelings and heartache following Anne's death, he wasn't so sure old wounds couldn't be reopened. His late sister-in-law had kept her obsession to be in the spotlight a secret from Nathan. And whatever the rest of the family had known or suspected, including Clint, no one spoke of Anne's audition trips out of town every time Nathan was away.

Until the car accident. A lot of angry words had been exchanged, accusations flung, rocking the Landers family's foundation to the core.

No, he wasn't about to kick up dust now. And for what, anyway? He liked Lila one hell of a lot. But nothing would come from whatever was happening between them. By the time they started shooting the sequel, finally giving her the role she wanted, he'd be only a passing memory for her.

Clint hoped he got off that easy. He'd never met a woman like her. And beauty didn't have a damn thing to do with it.

On second thought, that wasn't true. The fact that she was gorgeous did have something to do with what he liked about her. The real pretty girls he'd known had almost always centered their life on their looks. Lila wasn't vain, and she wasn't looking for a golden ticket to fame. She must've had doors flinging open left and right…for a price. Instead, she worked hard for her shot.

Fifteen minutes later, he pulled into the motel parking lot. Baxter's red convertible was conspicuously absent. Good. After yesterday's fiasco, it had gotten so Clint couldn't stand to look at the guy.

Clint knew from his earlier conversation with Lila some of the crew were still wrapping up at the set. Tomorrow everyone had the day off, including her. Clint had subtly warned his dad he might not make it home tonight and to not count on him for tomorrow.

After he'd parked the truck, he hit speed dial.

Lila answered on the first ring.

"I'm here," he said. "Are you ready or do you want me to come up?"

"Oh, definitely come up."

The excitement in her voice made his heart lurch. "I'll be right there."

He paused to check his teeth in the rearview mirror. Then took the elevator instead of the stairs and made sure his shirt was evenly tucked into his jeans.

Before he could knock she opened the door, wearing tight black jeans, a snug sweater and the best smile.

Then he noticed her hair. "What happened?"

"What do you mean?"

"Your hair…" Most of it was pinned up in back and on the left side. The rest fell to the right of her face. It looked as though the tips had been dipped in black paint.

"Oh." Lila laughed and motioned him inside. "I forgot." She closed the door. "I've been experimenting."

"With paint?"

"No." She stared at him as if *he* was crazy. "Extensions."

"Okay. I think."

Smiling, Lila took his arm and led him to the table and chairs in the corner. He sat without her asking.

She stepped back and freed the silky cloud of blond hair. Then she reached underneath and pulled out what looked like a miniature, black-tipped donkey's tail.

"See? It isn't really my hair. It's called an extension."

"Why?"

She shrugged. "It's as good a name as any, I suppose."

"Not what I meant. Why would anyone want to put that thing in their hair?"

"You'd be surprised," she said, laughing, and continued to pull out the weird-looking tails.

"You do that often?" he asked, realizing he might've sounded critical. "You know...wear that kind of stuff?"

"Not me. But I do use them in my job."

"I'm glad," he said. "Your hair is way too pretty to mess with."

"Thank you." She moved closer. Close enough that he could smell the warm sweetness of her skin. She stepped between his spread legs and put her hands on his shoulders.

Every muscle in Clint's body tensed.

"It occurred to me that we hadn't discussed what we're doing tonight."

"No." Clint cleared his throat. He'd had someplace in mind, but for the life of him he couldn't remember. "No, we haven't."

"So, I took matters into my own hands," she said, and with a single smile reduced him to a tongue-tied teenager. "Oh, wait. I'll probably forget, so I should tell you before we get started."

Get started?

His brain seemed to stop working. Lila was talking,

but he hadn't caught any of it. Somehow he equated the words to sex, and he couldn't make himself see it any other way.

"Okay," she said, looking disappointed. "I'll probably go. Obviously you don't have to."

He took a deep breath. "Go where?"

"Shadow Creek." She paused, frowning. "Spencer's ranch."

Clint waited expectantly.

"You didn't hear any of it, did you?"

"Guilty."

Lila grinned. "Erin and Spencer are having a barbecue tomorrow, and the whole crew is invited."

"A barbecue in December?"

"That's what I said." She shrugged. "Erin's a bigger wuss about the cold than I am, so I figure it can't be too bad."

Clint put his hands on her waist and watched the tip of her tongue sneak out and wet her lips. "Does that include Baxter?"

"He's away until Monday."

"If you're going, count me in," he said, feeling the slight sway of her body.

Her hair was tousled from shaking it out, and he sure hoped she'd let him mess it up some more.

"To be honest, it'll probably turn into a bitchfest about him. But we wouldn't have to stay long."

"Let's talk about tonight."

"Talk?" The corners of her moist lips tilted up. She leaned closer. "I had something else in mind."

"Show me."

Lila smiled, and the way she shifted made him think she was going to sit in his lap, but she reached across the table for a paper sack he hadn't even noticed. The movement caused his hands to slide over her round bottom. She didn't seem to care. He wondered how she'd feel about a light squeeze.

She leaned back before he could find out.

"I picked up dinner," she said. "I thought we could eat in and just... I don't know—" She lifted a shoulder. "Kick back."

"Ah, that's Marge's cooking. I can't believe I didn't smell it before now."

"You were too worried about my hair."

"Yeah, I had a couple other things on my mind." He didn't like that she'd moved back to open the bag, and he caught her hand.

"Such as?"

"Trying to figure out just how determined you are to wreak havoc with my willpower."

"I'm not doing it on purpose."

He tugged her closer, and she voluntarily planted her nice, firm bottom on his lap. Too late he realized he should've made a minor fly adjustment.

She squirmed a bit, trying to get settled. "Oh, you really are happy to see me," she said, her eyes widening.

Damned if he could tell whether she was teasing or not. For some reason he thought she might be genuinely surprised. The woman was a mass of contradictions. Maybe he was the problem. He'd never realized it before, but he had a lot of ideas about Hollywood and actors. None of them very good.

"Want to know what I would really, really like?" she whispered, her voice a soft purr.

Clint knew one thing for sure. Those big blue eyes of hers could get a man in all kinds of serious trouble. "What's that?"

LILA PRESSED HERSELF against his broad chest, seeking his warmth and strength, craving the comfort she found in his arms. Obviously she knew it was impossible to actually melt into him, but she could pretend.

Nothing about how she felt around Clint made sense. Maybe this was part of the overall grieving process over her old life. She missed the relationship she used to have with Erin, and she missed her family. And working on location for three months? It wasn't anything like she'd imagined. She didn't mind the hard work, it wasn't that at all...

Clint wrapped his arms around her, and she lifted her chin and smiled at him.

He brushed a kiss across her mouth. "I'm waiting."

"For?"

"You were going to tell me what you wanted." His gold-flecked eyes had darkened, mesmerizing her, pulling her deeper into the sensual mist.

He was turned on, no denying the bulge she felt under her backside. But his voice and actions were calm, controlled. If she said no, he would back up three feet. And then step back another two just to be sure she didn't feel threatened.

Clint was a gentleman, and she didn't use the word often or lightly. What made him interesting...he was also hot. Superhot. Or as Erin would say, hot as hell.

"Tell me the truth, Clint Landers. Women must fall for you all the time," she said, watching his brows rise. "How long does it usually take? Five minutes? Ten?"

"Never that long." His lopsided smile set off a flutter in her tummy.

Maybe Erin was right. There was just something about a cowboy.

He lowered his head until his breath danced along the line of her jaw. "You have something to tell me," he murmured, his voice deep and raspy, tickling the skin at the side of her neck.

A minute ago all she'd wanted was a kiss. "You," she whispered. "And me. Naked." She took a small nip of his ear. "In that bed over there."

She felt something stir under her butt, and a giggle slipped from her lips.

Clint looked at her with a half smile.

"Is that okay?" Lila asked, remembering the food was still warm but it wouldn't be later. "Are you hungry? Would you rather eat first?"

His gaze fell to her mouth, lingered, before he claimed it with a searing kiss. Lifting her in his arms, he stood as she clung to him, tightening her hold around his neck without the slightest misgiving over what they were about to do.

He laid her down gently, keeping the kiss intact until the last possible second. Lila was already breathing hard as if she'd been the one doing all the lifting. After unzipping her, he tried to peel her jeans down her hips.

Lila smiled at his frustration. She should've warned him they wouldn't be easy.

He narrowed his gaze. "What did you do? Spray paint this thing on?"

"They aren't called skinny jeans for nothing." She kicked off her leather ballet flats, intent on helping him. But he managed to get the job done just fine by himself.

Getting up on her elbows, she started to take off her sweater. At the rapt look on his face, she froze.

Clint's gaze traveled the length of her bare legs, then he leaned down and fingered the red silk triangle of her thong. "If I were to turn you over, I believe I'd have a real nice surprise."

"I believe you're right."

His sexy smile gave her goose bumps their own baby goose bumps. He sat on the edge of the bed and slipped a finger under the silk. Thank heavens she'd given herself a wax job last week. His exploration was getting a bit thorough…he grazed her clit and she let out a gasp.

His dark eyes glittered with satisfaction, and more. So much more. Lila didn't think any man had ever wanted her as intensely as Clint did in this very moment. Desire blazed hot in his gaze. A muscle worked in his jaw.

He slid a hand under her sweater. His palm grazed the skin between her ribs until he found a nipple and thumbed it through the silk of her bra. "This is like Christmas morning. I don't know which package to unwrap first."

"Then let me decide." She yanked his shirt from his jeans and heard a snap pop. It didn't stop her from reaching for his belt. The buckle was too tricky for her to do one-handed.

Clint stood and pulled up her sweater. She lifted her arms so he could tug it off all the way. He tossed it on the other side of the bed, his gaze sweeping over her and coming to rest on her face.

She could feel her cheeks heat. Not from embarrassment or anything like that. She was excited, happy, and so turned on her panties had already skipped the damp phase. All day she'd been distracted knowing tonight she'd be able to see more than his bare chest. And hoping she'd be allowed to touch him all she wanted.

He unsnapped his cuff and then started on the other sleeve. "You mind taking that off for me," he said, nodding at her bra.

"Since you asked so nicely." She reached behind

and found the hook quickly, then let the cups slide off slowly.

Watching her with hooded eyes, his lips parted. His nostrils flared. He'd unsnapped the front of his shirt but he just stood there, staring, barely moving.

Finally he leaned toward her, but she scooted over to the other side of the bed. "Take your shirt off."

He could easily reach her if he wanted. But his slow smile told her he'd concede this round, and he shrugged out of the soft wool shirt. When he sat on the edge of the bed to pull off his boots, Lila ditched the bra entirely and came up on her knees behind him. She dragged her hard nipples across his back as she placed a kiss on his shoulder.

Clint shuddered.

His skin was hot, feverishly hot, making her breasts prickle as she pressed against him. He yanked off the second boot and twisted around. His mouth claimed hers, the fierceness of his kiss pushing her backward.

He covered her left breast with his hand and fingered the tight nipple. His tongue continued to stroke and tease, keeping her off balance. She couldn't reach his buckle, but she wanted his jeans gone. Now.

The lofty thought blurred when he bowed his head and sucked a nipple into his mouth. The slightly rough texture of his tongue did amazing things to her sensitive skin. Firming his lips, he tugged hard at the rigid peak, and she arched upward. His swift reflex was the only thing that kept her from toppling over. His arm curled around her waist and held her tight.

It was too late. She was already falling, tumbling out of control into a bottomless pit of heat and longing with nothing to latch on to but Clint.

_11_

HIS TOUCH WAS MAGIC, his mouth as hot as the noon sun. Clint knew just where to apply more pressure and when to use his teeth and tongue. Lila promised herself she wouldn't be distracted. She'd get him naked. But then he moved his mouth to her other breast, and she lost track of her thoughts.

The moment he eased back she gathered her wits.

His lips were damp, his expression confused as he watched her scramble off the bed. She knelt in front of him and got to work hastily undoing his belt. His impressive erection made the zipper trickier.

Clint touched her hair. "Why don't you let me do that," he said, lifting her chin and brushing a kiss across her lips.

Of course she didn't want to hurt him, but she couldn't help rubbing her palm against his fly as he pulled her up.

He drew in a sharp breath and let out a shaky laugh.

Once he was on his feet, in a matter of seconds he was completely naked.

Tall and lean, he had no tattoos or visible scars. His skin had a healthy glow to it And she zeroed in on his tapered waist and narrow hips. His thick aroused cock. He was a tempting package of strong, virile male.

Anticipation shuddered through her.

For God's sake, she had to stop staring. Although he wasn't shy about checking her out while he dug into his jeans pocket.

She yanked back the covers.

He dropped some packets on the nightstand. Two or three of them, she couldn't tell, but she applauded his optimism.

When he tugged her closer, she eagerly wound her arms around his neck. His hands gripped her waist as he looked into her eyes.

"You're off tonight, right?"

"I am."

"No last-minute phone call asking you to run to the set."

"Nope." She shook her head. "I'm all yours."

"Yeah?" Something thrilling and sexy burned in his dark eyes.

"For the whole night."

"I like the sound of that." Reaching around, he cupped her butt. He squeezed and pulled her flush against him.

The searing heat of his arousal pressed hard into her skin. She felt the moisture that slicked the crown as he backed her up. Her legs met the side of the bed. The next thing she knew, she was lying on her back and he'd stripped off her thong.

Her startled gasp was part giggle. "Sneaky."

"We were taking too long."

"We have all night, remember?"

"Don't worry." His gaze swept over her legs and hips,

practically daring her to squeeze her thighs together. "I'll make good use of the time."

A tremor spiraled through her body.

He pressed his right knee into the mattress. Leaning over her, he parted her thighs and kissed her.

Right there.

Slowly, he exerted a gentle pressure before thrusting his tongue past the seam and grazing her clit.

Gasping, she bucked against his mouth.

She loved foreplay, but she wouldn't last like this for long.

Clint kept her thighs parted, his tongue breaking contact only once while he climbed completely on the mattress and settled between her legs. He looked up, his gaze drawn to her left breast. Reaching a hand to touch it, he kissed her lower belly, his dark eyes focused on her nipple. He rubbed his thumb over the jutting flesh, and she held her breath.

He moved his hand to the other breast and gave the tight bud a light pinch.

Lila moaned.

"Are you always this sensitive?"

She bit her lip and shook her head.

His brows furrowed. "Am I hurting you?"

"No." She lifted her shoulders off the mattress and caught his face between her hands. They looked at each other for a long moment before she slid her fingers into his hair and tugged at him, guiding his mouth to her breast.

He rolled his tongue over the distended nipple before it disappeared into his mouth. He sucked, blew some air on the damp flesh, then sucked again. She could tell he was holding back. Probably still worried she was too sensitive.

Clutching at his muscled arm, keeping his hand where she wanted it, she whispered, "Is that the best you can do, cowboy?"

His short, rumbling laugh vibrated against her skin and all the way to her core.

Clint did exactly as requested. And at the same time, inserted a finger inside her.

Lila jerked at the sly move. A moan mingled with laughter spilled from her lips. "Wait," she said.

He lifted his head, but kept his finger right where it was. "What?"

"I can't reach you."

Ignoring her, he bowed his head. Switching to her other nipple, he sucked it deeply. As he worked in a second finger, his thumb found her clit. She couldn't stay still, not with his thumb circling and circling, his fingers plunging in farther. But with every move, he stayed with her, increasing the pressure until want turned to a throbbing need.

She closed her eyes, squeezing them tight, willing her body to slow down. Not react so swiftly. But she'd already lost control. The ache for release was too great…

Her whimper of protest was cut short.

The orgasm hit her full force. It gripped her with the power of a tornado, tossing her around like a rag doll as the fire inside her flared. She opened her eyes to slits, but couldn't see through the red-hot haze.

Beneath her palm she felt a cord of muscle. Her fingernails were digging into Clint's arm. Unfazed by it, he stayed with her the whole time, easing back when it became too much, as if he had the ability to read her every move, her every moan.

Finally the inferno became soothing warmth that washed over her body in slow languid waves.

Her hands fell like lead weights to the mattress. She wanted to touch him, his shoulders and the muscles rippling with each tiny movement. She wanted to run her palms along the hard planes of his toned body. And she wanted to feel the long thick length of him, wrap her fingers around the smooth taut skin. But she couldn't seem to make her hands or arms work.

Clint shifted and claimed her mouth with a bone-melting kiss. "Hi," he said, his smile strained at the edges, his eyes dark with banked desire.

"Hi," she murmured, barely having enough breath to get out the tiny word.

He cupped the side of her face, and she turned her head to nuzzle his hand. A tremor passed through his body. Her shuddering response shot all the way to the soles of her feet.

His hair was mussed and his lips damp. He slid down to place a soft kiss on her inner thigh.

She widened her eyes, fully alert. He couldn't possibly—

He lapped at the moist, protective folds of her sex.

Squirming, she tried to clamp her thighs together. "Clint." Her mouth had gone dry. "Clint, stop."

His head came up instantly. "Too sensitive?"

"No, it's not that." Shifting to lie on her side, she caught his arm. "Come here," she said, patting the mattress.

Surprise flickered in his eyes, but he did as she asked and settled next to her. Stretched out on his side, elbow bent, he propped his head and faced her. Their eyes met and she smiled at him. But then she got distracted by his bulging biceps.

"Are you going to tell me what's wrong?"

"Hmm?" she murmured, staring at the bunched muscle until she couldn't stand it. She had to touch. "Nothing's wrong." She laid a hand on his arm. Beneath her palm, the rock-hard muscle tensed.

His arousal stirred against her tummy.

That's what she really wanted.

Reaching between them, she wrapped a hand around his hot hard length. One long stroke, and his groan nearly shook the bed.

She got in two more pumps before he grabbed her wrist, keeping her immobile, while he blindly reached behind and almost knocked over the lamp. Cursing under his breath, he finally had to release her so he could search the top of the nightstand.

He found a condom, managing to dodge her hand at the same time.

"Wait," she said when he tore the packet. "Not yet."

"Why?"

"Just give me a minute. Three minutes. That's all I'm asking for."

Clint looked thoroughly and adorably confused.

She slid down for a taste. Salty. Spicy. All male. She licked the head dry.

With another groan, his hands tangled in her hair. He started to pull her away, and then his hold slackened. He gulped for air. Whispered something too raw and broken for her to understand.

Closing her mouth around him, she sucked lightly at first, then harder. She moved her way down, stroking him with her tongue, but she only made it partway.

"No," he said, his voice hoarse. "Not like this."

Lila felt another tug at her scalp. This time he wasn't fooling around. Too bad. She flicked her tongue and slid down to the base.

"C'mon, Lila…" He cut off a groan and fisted a handful of her hair. "You're killing me here."

Reluctantly she released him. "I didn't make *you* stop."

He was already rolling on the condom. "Really?" he said with a cocked brow. "You're going to pout?"

"Maybe." Tilting her head to the side, she licked her lips. He surprised her by rising, making her gasp as he laid her back against the pillows and pushed her legs apart.

Slipping between them, he ran a finger along her slick wet lips. "Have anything more to say?"

Watching his nostrils flare, seeing how ready he was, her heart pounded out of control. "Please?" she whispered, struggling for air when he slid his finger in partway.

Clint leaned down for a kiss. The moment their lips touched, she felt him enter her. Just a little. He pulled back when her body tried to grip him.

She narrowed her eyes in warning.

He just smiled and rubbed her with the tip of his cock, teasing her, stroking her where she was most sensitive, small calculated movements, sliding up and down, in and out, and making her crazy.

And pushing her too close to another orgasm.

But he was torturing himself, too. She could see the strain in his face, the muscle flexing in his jaw. He wasn't going to last…

But then Lila wouldn't, either. He slipped a little ways inside her, and she rocked up to meet him.

Clint froze, his body tensing. His gaze seemed to scorch her to the core.

He thrust into her. Hard and deep. His muscled arms

shook with the effort of keeping his weight off her. He withdrew just a little, then surged into her again.

Their moans tangled and filled the room as Clint filled her, stretching her beyond the border of anything she'd experienced before.

"Ah, Christ," he murmured, and pulled her legs tightly around his hips.

She gripped him for all she was worth as he plunged inside her. He did it again and again, his hoarse groan echoing in her ears as she felt the first hint of her climax.

Clint's low primal cry was enough to trigger her release. Arching beneath him, she was beyond thinking, beyond speaking, beyond anything other than feeling him explode inside her. Or maybe it was her body that had burst into a million glittering pieces shooting into the darkness.

A tremor racked her all the way to her soul. Her lungs burned with the need for air. And yet she felt as if she were floating…

"Lila." Clint's ragged whisper penetrated the fog. He dislodged her legs from his hips.

She felt his arm slide beneath her shoulders, and he hauled her up against him, chest to chest. He put his other arm around her and before she knew it, he'd rolled onto his back, taking her with him, his cock still sheathed inside her.

Of course he wasn't hard anymore, but it amazed her that she could still feel his heft. All she seemed capable of was lifting her chin. He pushed back the tangle of hair that covered half her face, then slowly traced her bottom lip with his forefinger.

She sighed with contentment, not even trying to move. "I see you've done this before."

Clint smiled. "Yeah, a couple times."

"Good Lord. I think you've worn me out."

Her breathing was too shallow for her to be talking. She had to rest and regroup. She wouldn't turn down some water, either. A gallon would probably do it.

"Where are you going?" With a hand cupping her butt, he stopped her from rolling off.

"Water. The bathroom. And more water."

He nodded, looking so serious. "We're not done."

Lila laughed and shivered at the same time. "No, we aren't," she agreed and gave him a quick kiss before she rolled off him.

AFTER BEING AWAKE a few minutes, Clint finally opened his eyes. Moonlight poured in through the window past the partially open drapes. Careful not to disturb Lila, he barely moved. He sure was glad tomorrow was Sunday and neither of them had to work. Even if he did have to share her for part of the day.

She was laying on her side, curled toward him, one leg thrown over his, her pale hair spilling across his chest.

In a matter of weeks she'd be gone, and he didn't know if he'd ever see her again. She had a bright and busy future. Too bright to be sneaking off with a cowboy for a weekend here and there. Hell, that wouldn't be enough for him, anyway.

The notion was worrisome. That sort of thinking would only lead to trouble. So far they'd had sex twice since he'd arrived for their date. He glanced at the clock. It was 2:20 a.m. Technically, already Sunday. They'd stopped fooling around to eat cold fried chicken and cornbread. He smiled thinking about the staggering amount of honey she'd used to drown her cornbread.

The woman sure loved her sugar. Maybe that's what made her hair and skin smell so sweet. And man, the way she tasted…

Shit.

What was wrong with him, anyway? Having those sappy thoughts? He'd never been that kind of guy.

She snuggled deeper against his chest, and the flood of warmth that flowed through his body was unlike any other feeling he'd ever had.

"Are you awake?" she whispered.

"Sort of. You?"

Her laugh was husky with sleep. "What time is it?"

"Two-thirty-ish." Tightening his arm around her, he kissed her hair. Damned if he wasn't getting hard again.

Lila sighed. "It's Sunday. No setting the alarm. Yay."

"What time is the barbecue?"

"Around three. But I told Erin I'd go early to help."

Maybe he'd drop her off and run home, shower, change. "I should've brought extra clothes."

She lifted her head and looked at him with sleepy blue eyes. "Why didn't you?"

"I didn't want to jinx it."

"Jinx what?"

Clint touched the tip of her nose. "Don't give me that innocent look. Anyway, I should run home at some point. Won't take me long. I wonder what we should do in the meantime…" he said, cupping her breast.

She shivered and swelled to his touch. "Hmm, I wonder," she whispered, slowly stretching out on top of him.

12

THE WEATHER WASN'T half bad for a barbecue. Well, considering it was *December*, Lila thought. Red jumped to his feet and opened the patio door for her. Juggling two large platters, she smiled her thanks and braced herself before she stepped out onto the patio.

A light gust of cold air greeted her, but that wasn't the reason she paused by the door. She smiled as she watched Clint flip steaks and burgers on the massive stainless-steel barbecue. He looked right at home, sipping from a bottle of beer and keeping close tabs on the progress of the meat.

About half the crew had shown up. The wranglers were wandering around the barns and stable. Some of the guys were watching a televised football game in Spencer's den. With the exception of Rhonda, Davis and the new camera assistant sitting around a fire pit at the other end of the patio, the rest of the crew had gathered in the rec room to gripe about one thing or another.

Lila was having fun helping Erin in the kitchen. Mostly it was the other way around. Lila loved to cook and bake, and Erin was always much happier to have no part of it whatsoever.

Clint had dropped her off at Shadow Creek, zipped home and still arrived ahead of everyone else. Erin had put him to work assisting Spencer. The two men had hit it off right away, which made Lila stupidly happy. What did it matter? Sure it made for a more pleasant afternoon. But to expect anything beyond today? She knew better.

"Wow, you're in some serious like." Erin had come up behind her, a beer in each hand.

"No." Lila rolled her eyes and slid another peek at Clint. "Maybe." She sighed. "Okay, I'm pretty screwed."

Erin grinned. "Why? He's a good guy."

Clint must've heard them because he turned and smiled.

Lila smiled back. He returned his attention to the grill, and she sighed. "What difference does it make?" She'd lowered her voice. "I mean, I do like him and we're having fun. But you know how it is in this crazy business…" She looked her friend directly in the eyes. "What about you and Spencer?"

Erin blinked and took a sudden interest in the bottles she was holding. "Oh, here," she said, trying to pass a beer to Lila.

"You can't tell me you haven't been wondering what's going to happen once we wrap up here."

"Of course I have. But am I going to discuss it now? Here?" She glanced around, mostly for effect. "No."

"You always were a bad actress." Lila grabbed a bottle and twisted off the top.

"Never claimed to be one at all," Erin replied.

Clint glanced back at them. "The meat's done. You want to hand me that platter?"

"Coming right up," Lila said, and then to Erin, "To be continued."

"I can hardly wait."

Ignoring her, Lila moved close to Clint and kissed his jaw.

He lifted a brow in surprise.

No one had asked why he was here. Besides Spencer and Dusty, who worked at Shadow Creek, Clint was the only other outsider.

She took a whiff of the sizzling steaks. "Oh, my God, I think I'm going to faint." At his look of alarm, she grinned and set the beer aside. "These smell crazy good. How about I hold the platter while you transfer the steaks over?"

"What about the burgers?"

"I don't care what you do with those."

Clint laughed. Leaning closer as he reached for the tongs, he murmured in that low, raspy tone she loved, "I want to kiss you all the way into next Sunday." He straightened and returned to his normal voice. "Pick out a steak, and I'll set it aside for you. Medium is on the right."

She'd thought for sure he'd been about to bite her earlobe. "Thanks, now I'm one big goose bump, you rat."

His mouth curved in a self-satisfied, purely male grin. He glanced behind them before going to work filling the first platter. "Why do all these folks think I'm here?"

"Because Erin invited you."

"That's all?"

"I'm sure there's been talk…"

"You do realize you kissed me."

"On the jaw." She grinned and pressed her leg against his. "Only because I couldn't reach your mouth."

"Warn me next time. I'd be happy to cooperate."

"Hey, I didn't mean to desert you." Spencer's voice came from behind. "I got cornered by—"

Lila hastily moved away from Clint, as if she'd just been caught raiding the Christmas candy. She couldn't explain her reaction. Reflex?

"And now I'm interrupting." Spencer hesitated, even when Lila turned to smile at him.

"Of course you aren't. As a matter of fact, you're just in time." She held up the platter piled high with steaks. "Mind taking this to the kitchen?"

"No, ma'am. It's the least I can do after leaving Landers here to do the grilling."

Clint chuckled, and as soon as she'd lifted the second platter, he started loading that one, too. "This is a damn nice barbecue. Makes me wonder why I'm still using charcoal and an old barrel."

"Because you aren't lazy," Spencer said, laughing. "Want me to wait for that other platter?"

"Thanks, but I can manage," Lila said, but almost dropped it when Clint pushed the steaks to the side to make room for the burgers. It weighed a ton. "Didn't know you were feeding a whole regiment, did you?"

"Good thing I'm in the cattle business," Spencer said with a grin and started toward the door. "Clint, you want another beer?"

"Maybe later."

"Oh." Lila nodded to the bottle she'd taken from Erin. "That's for you. I took a couple sips."

"Thanks," he muttered, focused on scraping the grill with a spatula. "You know if there's anything else to go on here?"

"Erin didn't say." Lila could tell something was wrong, and she hated that she might've made things awkward between them. "I'll go ask."

He caught her arm as she turned. "I understand why you'd want to be cautious around the crew. I've got no problem with that," he said, and then with a self-deprecating smile added, "Not that you should care what I think."

"I'm not trying to downplay anything, but I knew you'd think that and I'm sorry. I can't tell you why I…" Lila sighed. "Half the guys have already hooked up with locals. It's practically a tradition when a movie's on location, but I never do, so…"

"It doesn't matter." He squeezed her arm, and while he tried to hide it, she caught his little satisfied smile. "Why don't you take that inside and find out if there's anything else for me to grill before I turn this off."

"Okay," she said, nodding. "Wait. What do you mean turn it off?"

"It's gas. No charcoal mess, just on, off, done. Plus it's hooked up to the line going into the house. I'm gonna steal the idea for the home I'm building."

Lila thought she'd heard wrong. "You're building a house?"

He glanced up, looking very much like a man who wanted to kick himself. It made her all the more curious. "I have plans to build. Just not at the moment."

"How exciting," she said, and meant it, if only for a second. A man usually built a house when he was ready to settle down. Start a family. Did he have a woman in mind? Clint had denied having a girlfriend, and she'd believed him. She still did. That didn't mean he wasn't narrowing down prospects. "Where will you build? Around here?"

He nodded. "You should get the meat inside before it gets cold."

"Oh. Right."

She hurried to the kitchen where Erin started firing questions at her. For a smart woman, Erin was terrible at coordinating cooking times. Lila was glad she was too busy to worry about anything but getting the food to the table without turning every dish into jerky.

Clint had done as instructed and undercooked the burgers and steaks so they could be finished in the oven. Spencer had thought of that little trick though, not Erin. Lila would've keeled over if her friend had put that much thought into anything related to cooking. But what really interested Lila was why Clint had urged her inside with the steaks. Obviously he'd regretted mentioning the house and wanted the subject dropped. And now she wondered why.

Dinner was a boisterous affair, everyone talking over everyone else as if they didn't live in one another's pockets. But finally the dishwasher was loaded, and most of the gang had settled on couches and chairs, or on the floor in the rec room. It took all of thirty seconds before the conversation turned to Baxter.

"Is the prick going to be around for the sequel, too?" Red asked just as Lila entered the room.

Clint immediately got up from the recliner he'd nabbed.

Lila motioned for him to sit back down. "We'll share," she said, and then sat on his lap.

Practically everyone in the room stared at her.

"Really, guys?" She swept her glare around. "I wish you'd paid this much attention when we needed help washing pots."

Clint's chuckle tickled her ear. She snuggled back against him, and he wrapped an arm around her as she got comfy.

Charlie cleared his throat. "I hope not," the grizzled wrangler said in his tobacco-roughened voice, referring to Baxter. "That kid's got as much sense as a hen's got teeth."

"Hell, that's giving him too much credit." Red looked at Erin as she and Spencer joined them. "Erin, you must know. Tell me that kid ain't hanging around for the sequel."

After a brief hesitation, she said, "Probably, he will."

"Probably?" Frowning, Red gave up his seat on the couch for Erin. "You don't know for sure?"

Spencer walked straight to the fireplace and took his time adding logs to the fire. He knew something. Lila had seen his jaw tighten before he'd turned his back to them. Obviously Erin had confided in him.

It was silly for Lila to feel hurt, but she did.

"Okay. Look…" Erin huffed an exasperated sigh. "He's a pain in the ass. I know that, and I'm not asking you to go out of your way to be nice to him—"

"Shiiit," the camera crew drawled in unison.

"Yeah, if I'm going outta my way," Red said, "it'll be to wrap his goddamn Beemer around his goddamn fat head."

Laughter took over. They sounded like a bunch of preschoolers. Normally Erin would've told them to shut up. Shrinking back against the couch, she looked as though she'd rather disappear.

She met Lila's eyes and quickly looked away.

"Baxter's scared of you," Tony said to Erin. "He wets himself every time you look at him. You're going to be first AD. Can't you give him the boot?"

Lila stared at her friend. Unlike everyone else, Lila wasn't waiting for her reply.

Holy crap.

Erin wouldn't look at her.

It didn't matter. Lila had already seen the telltale twitch. So tiny, it was easy to miss. For anyone who didn't know Erin inside and out.

The recent lack of enthusiasm, the avoidance, the short temper... Erin's behavior hadn't made sense. Exhaustion had nothing to do with it. What if it had something to do with the first AD's position Jason promised her? She'd sacrificed a year of her life for a shot at it.

No, that was too extreme. Jason wouldn't screw her over. He depended on her too much.

Now, Baxter, he'd been a problem from day one. Erin was angry about being saddled with him. Jason had forced the idiot on her in exchange for his uncle's money. Lila had assumed that after they wrapped, that would be the end of Baxter. Now, she wasn't sure what to think.

The timing had thrown Lila. Erin had met Spencer two months ago. And talk about falling hard. This thing with him wasn't a passing fling, so it had been easy to miss the real reason Erin's head wasn't in the game.

Baxter must be an even bigger problem than Lila had guessed. Had to be. But what was worse by far, Erin hadn't told her. Hadn't turned to Lila for comfort or help. And that cut went deep.

Clint's arm tightened around her. "Hey," he whispered, "you okay?"

"Fine." Her whole body had tensed, and her pulse ramped up. "Just tired."

"You want to go?"

"I think I do," she murmured, aware Erin hadn't looked at her even once.

THEY DROVE BACK to town mostly in silence. Clint felt helpless, something he'd just discovered he wasn't good at. He'd never been the controlling type, or maybe he'd just never been tested. Clint had pretty much run the Whispering Pines since the day after he'd quit college. Lucky for him, the operation ran exactly how he wanted it to run. On the not so lucky front, the ranch had become the sum total of his life.

Right now, he'd do just about anything to get Lila to smile.

Except he didn't think there was one damn thing he could say or do that would cheer her up.

She stared out the window at the semidarkness, fidgeting with her hands, and surely setting some kind of record for sighs per minute. He doubted she realized she was making a sound.

"I'll go beat up Baxter if you want me to," he teased, and she turned, eyes widening. "Say the word."

Her unexpected grin lit up the darkest corner of his soul. "I don't care about Baxter."

"Something sure has gotten you down."

With another sigh, she turned to look out the window again. Not many stars had made a showing yet.

"You know what we could do," he said. "Drive over to Kalispell and look at the Christmas lights. Not just downtown, either. I heard some of the neighborhoods go all out."

"Oh, that would be fun," she said, "but not tonight. I hope that doesn't disappoint you."

"Nope. I just want to see you happy."

"Oh, I'm sorry. You were great about going to the barbecue, and now I'm being a spoilsport."

"I had a good time, and I'm glad I met Spencer. Interesting guy."

Lila nodded. "I don't think I could've picked anyone

more perfect for Erin. At least that's going well, so—"
She stopped short. "So that's great."

Clint wished she would've finished what she'd
started to say. Hell, he wished for a lot of things when
it came to Lila.

She surprised him by reaching over and brushing a
lock of hair off his forehead.

"I didn't mean to startle you," she said, snatching
her hand back.

"But in a good way."

"Yeah?"

He heard the smile in her voice, and he pulled the
truck off to the side of the highway.

"What are you doing?" She straightened in her seat.
"Is something wrong—?"

His aim was bad in the darkening cab. Their lips
met clumsily. They both smiled, and then everything
lined up perfectly: lips, tongues, lightly nibbling teeth…

He touched her hair, savoring the feel of the soft,
silky strands. Her lips were soft, too, and so was her
skin. He'd given up trying to understand how it could
feel like velvet and satin at the same time. Her whispered sighs floated into the night.

Two hours ago he'd cut himself off, drank his
last beer. But it was Lila and her seductive scent he
should've been worried about. The sweet smell of her
skin intoxicated him like no alcohol ever had. It made
him think foolish thoughts. Made him long for things
he had no business wasting energy on.

Knowing he could never have a woman like her for
keeps didn't dull the want.

They were five minutes from town. He wasn't crazy
about them sitting there, making out on the side of the
highway, but there was no way of telling if she planned

on inviting him to her room. Just coming out and asking didn't feel right.

They broke apart for some air.

"Let's run away for a week," he said, the words tumbling out of his mouth before he knew it.

"Let's." She laughed. "Wait. Only a week?"

"A month?"

"Keep going."

"Don't tease me, Lila. That's not funny."

With a wistful sigh, she leaned in for another kiss. Her soft lips sent a jolt straight to his groin. "Who's teasing?"

His heart lurched. Why was he being so stupid? Just because he'd seen another side to her. Yeah, he'd been surprised when she'd taken over the kitchen the minute she arrived. The way she'd issued orders and went right to work sorting through pots and casserole dishes reminded him of his mom on holidays. The kitchen turned into a well-oiled machine, and everyone knew who was boss.

He doubted Lila was the only actor who knew how to cook, but he'd expected her to be more like Erin, who'd clearly been out of her comfort zone. She was a mini-tyrant on the set, but in the kitchen she waited like a puppy for Lila's instructions.

He caught a set of headlights in the rearview mirror. "Guess we'd better go."

Lila glanced back. "Where?"

"Anywhere you want."

She smiled. "How about Canada?"

Clint chuckled. "A minute ago I couldn't get you to go to Kalispell."

"Canada is less than two hundred miles away, right?"

The small SUV sped past them, and he eased the

truck back onto the highway. "Yep, to the border," he said, not sure what to make of her almost desperate tone. "With nothing but nowhere land on both sides."

"Sounds perfect," she said softly and kind of wistfully again. "Except we're going back to town, aren't we?"

He looked at her. "You're serious?"

She smiled. "Jeez. Would you listen to me?" she said, shaking her head. "Being so selfish. You probably have a million chores to catch up on."

No, he was the selfish prick. Something was really bothering her, and his mind kept rebounding to sex. He saw the turnoff for Cherry Point and made a split-second decision.

13

THE TRUCK BOUNCED over a pothole. Lila threw a hand out and clutched the dashboard. "Where in the world are we going?"

"Cherry Point. The best high school make-out spot in three counties. At least it used to be." Damn, he was old.

"Cherry Point. Really?" She squinted past the windshield into the gathering darkness.

"Hey, I didn't make up the name."

"I would've forgiven you if we're going to make out."

"I'm sure we'll get around to that, but first—"

Her phone buzzed.

"You might want to get that," he said, slowing down. "I can't say we'll have a signal for long."

She peered into the forest of tall, dense pines all around them. "You really are going to take advantage of me, aren't you? Or maybe I'll take advantage of you. Either works for me—or both."

Clint smiled. "Is that a yes or no on taking the call?"

"What? Oh." She shook her head, her pale hair catching the moonlight and shimmering like it had been sprinkled with fairy dust. "I know who it is. It can wait."

"I don't mind getting out and giving you privacy."

She smiled and brushed the stubborn lock off his forehead again.

He'd brought her here to talk. His brain understood, but his body responded to even her briefest touch. Talk first, he reminded himself, then…

Well, that depended on a lot of things that he'd be a fool to forget.

He stopped the truck and brought her fingers to his lips. He kissed the tip of each one before pressing his mouth to her soft palm.

"Here?" A shudder shook her shoulders as she glanced around at the eerie shadows. "This is the famous Cherry Point?"

"No. Farther into the woods."

"It's kind of spooky."

"I would never take you anywhere dangerous," he said, and she looked at him. "But if this is making you nervous, we'll turn back."

"I know you wouldn't." She curled her fingers around his hand.

"I'd always keep you safe." He touched her cheek, stroking his thumb down the velvety softness. Feeling self-conscious all of a sudden, he stopped. "Does it bother you that my hands are rough?"

"No." She gripped his wrist, preventing him from lowering his hand.

"But you're so soft…"

"I like it."

"But—"

"Clint." She moved closer. "I like it when you touch me. And when you kiss me," she said, leaning close enough he felt her breath on his chin.

His cock jerked against the denim fly.

Her lips grazed his.

"Shit," he muttered, not meaning to say it out loud. "Sorry."

"It's okay."

"I didn't bring you here for this." He ordered himself to stand down, to use his brain and not his dick.

"I don't understand."

"I wanted us to talk."

She sank back. "Talk about what?"

"Look, I know something's bothering you. And I figured out here where it's dark, you might be more comfortable and—" He shrugged, relaxed his clenched jaw. "If you need someone to listen, or if there's some way I can help…" Gritting his teeth, he scrubbed at his face. "I don't know what I'm saying. I'm way out of my depth here."

Lila's soft laugh loosened the knot coiling in his gut. "Well, sure, you used the word *talk*. With a woman. Ever done that before?"

"Never."

"That's what I thought." Her grin was contagious.

"Don't poke fun," he said. "It's a humbling experience."

"Yes, but now you've made it over the biggest hurdle. The first time is always the hardest."

Clint laughed. She got that wrong. The hardest part was fixing to bust through his fly at this very moment. Trying to ignore it was no picnic, either.

Her phone rang again.

Lila pulled it out of her pocket as if she dreaded the call. "It's my sister," she said, her tone flat. "She wants to know when I'm coming home for Christmas. I'll just be a minute." She sighed before answering. "Hey, Brit, what's up?"

Her voice had changed in an instant, even her expression had transformed. As if she'd slipped into a different role.

"Just flurries, mostly. I heard we might get slammed next week." She paused. "I think you should go shopping without me."

Clint did her the courtesy of turning his face away. Naturally she didn't care that he could hear her side of the conversation. Lila was acting now. Controlling the inflection of her voice. Her sister couldn't tell a damn thing about her mood. Of course, neither could he. Whatever Lila was feeling was locked tight inside.

Nathan's first wife popped into his head. It occurred to him that Anne had used her acting skills to keep his brother in the dark about a big part of her life. He had no idea why she'd been so secretive, but finding out the truth after her death had nearly done Nathan in.

Lila sure didn't owe Clint anything. They barely knew each other. He couldn't help wondering, though, if things were different, would he worry she was hiding her true feelings from him?

"I didn't say that, Britney. I can't promise, but that doesn't mean I'm not trying." A small crack in her voice had her shifting in her seat. "You know what... I should've mentioned now isn't a good time. How about I call you tomorrow?"

Clint stared out his window at a curious young buck standing several feet away in the brush.

"I am not." Lila let out a sound of frustration. Apparently she'd quit holding back. "I'm on a date, okay? Oh, God. Fine. Clint?" She held the phone near his face. "Would you please say something to my sister?"

"Um, sure. Hi, Lila's sister... Britney. Right?"

A high-pitched squeal nearly pierced his eardrum.

Lila quickly took back the phone. "Happy?" She bit off a giggle. "Shut up. Goodbye."

Britney's excited voice was still audible as Lila disconnected. She stuffed the phone in her pocket, then pulled it back out.

"I need to turn it off or she'll drive me nuts." She took care of that and said, "Where were we? You said something about making out?"

Clint shook his head. "I'm starting to worry. Everyone is shocked to see you with a man. I hope you're not one of those black widow serial killers."

Grinning, she reached over and cupped the back of his neck. "You found me out," she said, pulling him toward her. "Now I'm going to kiss you to death."

"You sound awfully chipper when you talk about murder," he said, well aware that he'd stopped trying to get her to open up to him. He felt her smile against his lips. And he did something he'd been *dying* to do all afternoon.

Clint slipped his hand under her sweater and cupped her breast. Her nipple was hard beneath the silky barrier of her bra. With a quiet whimper, she shifted so that it was easy for him to dip a finger into the cup. Soft, soft skin surrounded the stiff nipple. A pale pink normally, by now it would have turned three shades darker.

He remembered every detail from last night. How her lips and nipples flushed as her arousal heightened. And how she bit her bottom lip a lot, trying to stifle her loud moans of pleasure. When that hadn't worked, she had put a hand over her mouth. Clint had enjoyed peeling her fingers away and thrusting his tongue between her lips, kissing her long and hard until they'd both gasped for air.

After he'd worked her bra strap down her shoulder

a bit, he managed to lower the cup and free her breast. The creamy flesh almost filled his hand. She was the perfect size, not too big, and all her, nothing fake or unnatural about the feel as he kneaded gently.

He wanted to put his mouth on her. Flick his tongue quick and light the way he knew she liked it. He had offered to listen if she needed to talk. Nothing more he could do on that front. It was up to her.

Avoiding the gearshift, she pressed against him, parting her lips and welcoming his tongue with a light suction and then meeting him stroke for stroke. The sweet taste of her mouth lured him closer, deeper. The warm scent of her skin, the firm, silky feel of her round breast...

Clint stiffened against the speed and intensity of his body's response. The woman was going to send him straight into cardiac arrest.

She arched into his palm and moaned, the sound coming from somewhere at the back of her throat. Her nails dug into his forearm. Heat surged through his body. Distorted his senses. Almost made him forget they were sitting in his truck in the cold night air. As far as he was concerned, they could stay right where they were and wait for summer.

He broke the kiss and dragged in a lungful of air, hoping that would clear his head. What he got was a strong whiff of her arousal.

Jesus.

Lila cupped his fly.

He froze, braced himself. His cock throbbed. He wanted to believe he had more self-control now than he'd had as a teenager. But damn. Maybe she really was trying to kill him. It wouldn't be a bad way to go.

She applied more pressure and started rubbing him,

which caused way too much of a ruckus inside his body. He clamped a hand around her wrist, and she stopped.

"We should've gone straight to the motel," she murmured and licked his chin up to his lips.

He leaned back, but she just kept licking any part of him she could get to. Finally he put enough distance between them.

"Spoilsport," she said, sinking back. "You can let go of my wrist."

"I don't trust you."

Her lips lifted in a devilish smile. "Why?"

"You can't touch me like that."

"Like what?"

"C'mon, Lila, you can't expect me not to—"

Her free hand came at him like a bullet.

"Like this?" she asked, pressing her palm against his cock, rubbing up and down, the thick denim offering no protection.

He groaned through gritted teeth. "Goddamn it, Lila." The curse had slipped out, but she'd get no apology this time. He was about to explode with frustration. She was going to make him come, and he didn't want that. Not now. "Can we wait until we get to town?"

"Um…" She paused. "No."

Clint blocked her next move. Good to know he still had his high school football reflexes.

Calmly she reached around him and cut the engine. "Thanks," she said, looking him in the eyes, "for offering to listen. I need this more."

Absorbing the meaning behind her words, he nodded slowly.

Dumb cowboy.

Took him long enough to get it. He was her distraction. Not that he felt *used*. Or regretted any part he played in her life this last week. But he wasn't special. He'd seen how the men in the crew had eyed him. That and knowing she rarely dated had turned his head some.

For whatever reason, she felt safe with him, felt confident that he understood this was just a fling. That it would all come to an end the day the movie wrapped and she left. Or it could end tomorrow.

He gazed into her expectant eyes. "Is that so?"

Smiling, she nodded and reached for his fly.

"Hold on." He took her hand and entwined their fingers. "I didn't say you could have your way with me."

Laughter burst from her lips.

He cupped her chin and brought her face closer. "Kiss me."

She was still trying to lose the grin as she leaned forward. He covered her mouth with his, then slowly turned up the heat while he moved his hand to find her zipper. Her tongue circled his, then swept around his mouth demanding he join the dance. The kiss was supposed to sidetrack her, not him.

He had her unbuttoned and unzipped fairly quickly, and then felt her tremble. "You cold?"

"Mostly just excited."

Clint smiled at her honesty and paused to restart the engine and adjusted the vents to get the heat circulating. "Think you'd be warm enough without your sweater?"

Lila stared at him, her eyes widening as she nodded. The determined temptress was gone, leaving behind a young woman who looked unsure of herself. This wasn't the first unguarded moment he'd glimpsed of Lila. But he had a feeling these brief displays of vulnerability were rare.

He waited a few moments, but she didn't whip off her

sweater. Guess it was up to him. The space was tight, so it was awkward, but he managed to lift the sweater over her head.

Next Clint sprung the front clasp of the bra, and she did her part by letting the straps slide off her shoulders. Her smooth ivory skin glowed in the moonlit cab. The tips of her breasts were a dark rose, just as he'd expected. He touched the right one.

"Wait." Shivering, she barely got the word out. "What about you?"

He pushed her hair aside and kissed her neck. "What about me?" he murmured, and trailed his lips to her throat. Her little whimper spurred him on. Using the tip of his tongue, he traced the ridge of her delicate collarbone.

Her head fell back, and she made a soft contented sound.

Sucking her nipple into his mouth, he slipped a hand inside her jeans.

Lila inhaled with a quick shallow gasp. "Clint."

His name fell from her lips in a breathy whisper. An earthy muskiness laced her sweet scent, and a surge of lust shot through his veins. She bucked against his hand. He felt the tension slowly ease from her muscles.

He parted her with his fingers and slid them into her wet heat. Her clit had swelled. He thumbed it as he pumped his fingers in and out.

The sound of their ragged breathing filled the cab.

"Clint, what are you— Oh… God—" She'd brought her head partway up, then let it fall back against the headrest with a thump.

He smiled.

She'd said she needed this, and he was happy to give

it to her. Hell, he'd give her anything she wanted, anything that he was capable of providing, anyway.

For now, he hoped it would be the best damn climax she'd ever had—well, one of the best. What happened last night while he'd been inside her... He didn't think it was just his ego.

And after the fireworks, he was going to drop her off at the motel and then go straight home to talk to his dad. Put his mind at ease. Clint would let him know he was ready to take over the ranch. Why wait until after Christmas? What else did he have in his future besides the Whispering Pines?

Not Lila. No matter how much he fantasized or tried to read things into her sweet smiles and soft looks. This fling was just that to her. He was merely a stop on her bullet train to a big and glamorous life. And he sure as hell couldn't complain because she'd never led him to believe otherwise.

Giving his dad his word meant a lot to Clint...enough to clear the muck in his head. There'd be no more room for wishful thinking.

After that was done, he planned on spending every free minute he could with Lila. Until they'd screwed each other's brains out and he'd no longer have the capacity to understand she'd soon be gone forever. Almost like she'd never been there in the first place.

14

LILA WAS WORRIED. Definitely about Erin, that had never gone away. But now she was fretting over Clint, too. He parked the truck near the entrance of the motel. Baxter hadn't returned, or at least his car wasn't in the lot.

"Are you sure you don't want to come up?" She met his gaze. "I can return calls later. Or even tomorrow."

He smiled. "You sure do get a lot of calls and texts."

Her sister first, then her mom had called, and then Erin had texted. All of them multiple times. "Did that ruin the mood for you?" Lila asked.

"No." Clint laughed. "No," he repeated, shaking his head, then he leaned closer and kissed her lips.

He didn't linger, probably afraid of giving her the wrong idea. It was clear he wanted their date to end. She'd really hoped he would spend the night with her.

"Most of it is your fault," she said. "Everyone was calling because of you."

"What did I do?"

"Besides give me an orgasm that nearly blew my head off?" She sighed. "You think I'm selfish. But I tried getting you to—"

"I don't think you're selfish." Clint took her hand.

The light squeeze he gave it felt oddly platonic, but she liked the lopsided smile. "If I recall, I was the one who drove that particular cattle drive."

That made her laugh. "Interesting euphemism. Did you just think that up?"

"Come on," he said with another unsatisfactory squeeze. "I'll walk you to your door."

He got out of the truck, so she had little choice, other than to sit there by herself.

Clint opened her door and held it while she slid out. She couldn't help but see that he was hard, just as aroused as he'd been fifteen minutes ago. Would he still be that turned on if she'd done something wrong?

They headed for the entrance, his hand brushing against hers. It seemed he was about to take it. She saw his hesitation as clear as day.

She stopped. They both turned and faced each other. "Clint—"

"Look—" he said at the same time, then gestured for her to speak first.

Her cell phone chirped. She jerked it out of her pocket.

"Oh, shut up." She should never have turned the darn thing back on. Easy enough to fix. Her palms were damp, she realized, as she returned the phone to her pocket and looked up to find Clint studying her face.

"I think we have the same thing on our minds," he said and put his hands on her shoulders. "The timing sucks. Much as I would rather be going to your room with you, I have something very important to do. It concerns the ranch, which I've gladly neglected for nearly a week…" He smiled and lifted her chin when she slumped with guilt. "Something I plan on doing a lot more of, if you let me. But I have this one obligation I can't ignore. I realize now that I should've told you as soon as I remembered."

Relief washed over her. "Then go. I can get to my room just fine."

"I can at least walk you to your—"

"We'll probably start making out in the elevator."

"Good point." His frown was just too adorable. "Any chance I can see you tomorrow night? I don't care how late."

"Absolutely." She stretched up on her toes and kissed him. "Now, go."

His body no longer seemed tense as he pulled her into his arms. Then they started kissing, more passionately than they should in a public place. She pushed him away.

"What?" he murmured hoarsely.

"You have to go."

"Right." He reached for her again, but she'd stepped back. "God, you tempt me…"

"That's why I'm saying goodbye." She gave him a small wave as she backed toward the door. Mostly because he tempted her too. Clint made everything else so easy to forget.

Lila didn't have the responsibility of a ranch to run, but she had a duty to the film, to her career, and she owed Erin. They'd made a pact. They were in this rotten business together, for better or for worse. But even that didn't concern Lila at the moment.

When he didn't move, she turned and hurried into the motel. Once she was in her room, without even washing off her makeup or changing into her nightshirt, she called her friend.

"You didn't have to call back tonight," Erin said as a greeting. "Are you with him?"

"No," Lila said, sitting on the edge of the bed and slipping off her flats. "And we're not going to talk about Clint."

"Did something happen between you guys?"

"We're fine. It's us, Erin. Something's happened that you're not telling me," Lila said on an exhale. "And I won't pretend it's not killing me. Not anymore."

Erin allowed silence to stretch, and then she sighed. "We'll talk. But not on the phone. Tomorrow, okay?"

"That isn't fair."

"I'm not putting you off. I promise you. And please trust me that everything will be okay. But tomorrow would be better."

Lila agreed, disconnected and fell back against the pillows.

Her friend could assure her they'd talk, but she couldn't know that everything would turn out okay. Lila had a strong feeling that wouldn't be the case. And God, how she wished Clint were here to help her forget. But he was right. They tempted each other, in so many ways, and Lila sure didn't need to lose sight of her career, her future, not when she was so close.

Foolish her, she'd begun to think Clint just might be the one man she didn't want to let slip away. And yet she'd only known him a week.

One short week.

On top of that, it was the holiday season, and she was emotional about not being able to go home. That explained so much. It was for the best he wasn't spending the night, she thought, rolling over to bury her face in the pillow. Because with so much going on already, she was starting to seriously doubt her judgment.

CLINT WAS SURPRISED to see the office light on as he parked the truck. It was 9:20 p.m. He figured his dad would still be up, but not working on ranch business. It was the only time he used the office, and that was a rare occasion.

Guilt slammed Clint. Shit. He really had been neglecting his duties if his dad felt the need to step in, though he was the one who'd urged Clint to take some time off.

Not in the mood to run into his mom or grandmother, he skipped going through the house and walked to the outside entrance to the office. They never kept the door locked. He paused for a brief knock so he wouldn't startle his dad.

He was sitting behind the old oak desk with the middle drawer open and frowning. "Hi, son," he said, glancing up. "You're home early." He shoved aside a stapler and box of paper clips. "Do we have any tape in here?"

"What kind of tape?" Clint sat in the leather chair across from the desk. He wasn't used to the view from this side. Damn, they had a lot of books crammed together on the built-in shelves.

"You know…the kind your mom uses to wrap presents."

"Ah. I don't think so. Isn't there some in Mom's junk drawer?"

"I looked." Clearly agitated, he continued rifling through the desk. "She must've put it somewhere else. Probably with her wrapping paper."

"What do you need it for?"

"To wrap her Christmas present."

"You bought her something?"

His dad narrowed his eyes. "Yes, I did. Just like I've

done in the past. So, I'll thank you not to make it sound like I don't give your mom presents."

Clint laughed. "I meant it's not a vacuum cleaner or new washer. Not if you're going to wrap it."

"Wise guy. I bought tickets for a Caribbean cruise," he said, and Clint's jaw dropped. "You bought your gal anything yet?"

"You know Kristy and I broke it off months ago."

"I'm talking about the other gal," his dad said with a small smile.

"Don't have a gal, and I don't know what you're talking about."

"The young lady you spent last night with, Clint. I didn't expect I'd have to spell it out for you."

Clint sighed, wishing like hell he'd waited until tomorrow. "This is a different time, Pop. I like Lila," he said, not keen on discussing the topic with his old man. "I like her a lot. But she's not…mine."

"Why? Because she has something to do with that movie they're shooting near Blackfoot Falls?"

Clint nodded. "She's part of the crew, and when they're finished, she'll be gone."

He'd given up the search and was putting all his energy into frowning at Clint. "You know that for sure?"

"It's her job, Pop. I'm sure." Clint straightened. "Look, I wanted to talk to you. About me taking over. No point in waiting till after Christmas. We both know the answer. I'm honored you have faith in me."

"Faith in you?" He shoved a hand through his salt-and-pepper hair. "We still have the Whispering Pines because of you. I'm real clear about that," he said, when Clint shook his head. "I've always been a lousy businessman. I know my cattle, though. Just wish I'd had enough sense to let someone else handle the business end early on. Your mom's smart about that sort of thing. I was young, newly married and had too much ego to get her involved."

Clint rubbed his jaw. Sounded familiar.

"What's that grin for? Your old man was young once."

"Weren't we all?"

Doug Landers snorted a laugh. "Hell, you're still a pup. Smart as a whip, though, I'll give you that. You knew everything about auctions and keeping the books well before you went off to college. And even the cattle... Don't you tell your brother I said this, but you've always been a better cattleman than Nathan. He's good with horses."

Clint chuckled. "Come on, Pop. Give me an early Christmas present. Let me tell him you said that. You can be there to see his face."

"Yeah, go ahead, start a war. Your mom would love that." His smile faded as he looked solemnly at Clint. "What I'm getting to is this... I'm not accepting your answer. Not yet." He held a hand up when Clint started to protest. "Obviously I'm not questioning your ability. But you were right to ask for time to think it over. And I believe you still have some thinking to do."

"I don't understand what brought this on," Clint said, his insides clenching. "But I'm telling you that I'm—" He leaned back, not sure if he felt ashamed or offended. "You think I've been neglecting my job—"

"Hell, no. I told you to take time off, didn't I? Anyway, we have good men living in that bunkhouse," he said, jabbing a finger in that direction. "No reason you should be here 24/7. Not to mention you can handle the job with one arm tied behind your back. Your mom and I just want you to be sure. That's all."

Swiftly losing his sense of humor, Clint sighed. "I'm telling you I'm sure. I want to run the Whispering Pines. A Landers has held the reins for over a hundred years." Why had he said that? It had no bearing on anything. He was tired. Maybe his dad had mistaken weariness for uncertainty. "My decision has nothing to do with Seth acting out or Nathan having his own ranch to worry about. I'm telling you I'm ready."

"Good." His dad stood, and Clint exhaled. "I expect you'll still be ready in three weeks."

"Dad…"

He walked around the desk and stopped at the door. "Do me a favor, son. Pick me up some of that tape next time you're in town."

"I don't know when that'll be," Clint lied, feeling like a defiant teenager. Idiot.

"No rush." His dad tried hiding a smile. "It can wait until you go shopping for that present."

SOMETHING HAD HAPPENED on the set. Lila didn't know the specifics, only that the problem was big enough that Erin could weasel out of their talk and force half the crew to take an early lunch. Which sucked so bad because the day was already crawling.

Lila turned to go back inside the trailer when she thought she saw Clint's truck. She didn't think they needed him today, but he could be delivering horses. Straining to see around the corner, she nearly fell off the step.

"Looking for someone?"

The sound of his deep voice sent an army of goose bumps marching down her arms. She spun to face him, almost losing her balance, but he caught her by the waist.

"Someone tall, dark and handsome, as a matter of fact." She paused as he gave her the exaggerated eye roll that never failed to make her grin. "But you'll do," she added.

"You're in a good mood," he said, releasing her. "Filming must be going well today."

"Oh, no, it's a complete mess. They're at a standstill." She smiled at his puzzled expression. "I'm happy to see you," she said, considering sneaking in a kiss. "God, you're wearing your hat. Have I told you how much I love that Stetson? On you. Not the hat by itself."

Clint laughed.

"Did you get your business taken care of last night?"

"Yeah." He lifted the Stetson and resettled it on his head, looking beyond her toward the set. "Everything's fine."

"Did they call you to come today?"

He shook his head. "I had something to pick up in town and figured I'd stop by. You eating lunch with Erin?"

"We had plans to meet, but I doubt I'll see her for a while," she said, glancing toward the set. Baxter was headed their way. "Oh, great." She quickly turned back to Clint, who looked equally thrilled to see the moron.

Clint's jaw was set, his gaze fixed. Neither of them spoke. She braced for impact.

"What are you doing away from the set?" Baxter asked Clint. "They need you over there by the—" He waved a hand, clueless as usual. "Whatever they call it."

Clint's straight face dissolved, and he let out a laugh.

"They're not using him today, Baxter," Lila said, so sick of his obvious attempts to separate them. "Didn't you read the call sheet?"

His evil glower startled her, but she held firm and glared back.

"Jason and I want something for lunch." He challenged her with a dark look she'd never seen before.

"Okay," she said, shrugging. "You know where the craft service is set up."

"We're sick of that shit. Make yourself useful, go pick something up at the diner."

She opened her mouth to remind him *he* was Jason's gofer, not her. But she saw the anger in Clint's face and reconsidered.

Better not throw gas on the fire, she decided.

Baxter frowned at her outstretched palm. "What?"

"Money and the keys to your car."

Baxter scowled. "Don't you have money?"

"Nope." She waited, wiggling her fingers. "Hurry up, I don't have all day."

He pulled some bills out of his pocket and passed them to her, while he dug for his keys.

"You don't need his car," Clint said, pressing a hand to the small of her back. "I'll drive you."

"Thanks."

Baxter didn't like that at all. She tried not to let her glee show.

"Wow, a hall pass I hadn't expected," she said as they started walking. "Nice."

Clint still looked as if he wanted to rearrange Baxter's face. "What the hell is his problem?"

She shrugged. "He's jealous." It was a short walk to his truck. She glanced back a couple times, hoping to see Erin. Lila had been ready to have that talk. Since that wasn't possible at the moment, this wasn't a bad way to spend the time.

Although, she'd warned herself about relying too much on Clint.

He turned onto Main Street, and she looked at the crumpled bills. "Awesome. There's enough here for us to have lunch, too."

Clint chuckled. "How about I buy you lunch?"

"Actually I'm not hungry. Where are we going?"

"You tell me."

"Okay, the Food Mart."

Clint looked at her. "Have you had their ready-made sandwiches?"

"They're terrible. Jason will hate it." She smiled at his confusion. "Jason would never tell Baxter to send me to get lunch. That's part of Baxter's job description."

He kept driving, a smile slowly curving his mouth. "You can look so angelic. But you really are a little devil, aren't you?"

"When it comes to Baxter? Oh, yeah."

The parking lot wasn't crowded. Clint found a spot close to the front. As Lila slipped out, she caught a brief glimpse of herself in the side mirror and laughed.

"What?" he asked, coming around to hold the door. He was unfailingly polite. And not just with her. He always held a door for any woman.

"I forgot about this purple extension." She lifted it away from her own hair. "You didn't say anything."

"I've rearranged my expectations when it comes to you."

Lila waited for him to close the door. "I'm not sure if that's good or bad."

He surprised her by taking her hand. "Is this okay?" he asked, glancing at their entwined fingers as they walked toward the entrance.

"It is with me." She smiled so big her cheeks hurt.

Her parents would adore Clint. She squeezed his hand tighter.

He squeezed back. "Mom?"

"What did you say?" Laughing, Lila glanced up at him.

Clint wasn't looking at her. He'd stopped and was staring at a short, middle-aged woman with sparkling hazel eyes and the same olive skin coloring as Clint. "What are you doing here?"

The woman glanced from Clint to Lila and then at their joined hands. She smiled. "Shopping."

"Right." Clint released Lila's hand. "What's wrong with Bill's Food Town? Other than being thirty miles closer to home."

"Aren't you going to introduce me to your friend?" Mrs. Landers was studying Lila, but in a friendly way.

"Lila Loveridge meet Meryl Landers, my nosy mother."

"Oh, hush," Mrs. Landers said, sending him a reproving look.

Grinning, Lila extended her hand. "I'm so happy to meet you."

"I confess to being a bit starstruck," Mrs. Landers said as she accepted Lila's handshake. "I usually do shop at the Food Town in Twin Creeks, but I was hoping to see someone famous."

"Oh, we don't have any really big names. But I bet you've heard of Dash Rockwell and Penelope Lane."

"And you," Mrs. Landers said. "My goodness, I can't believe Clint has been keeping you a secret. You can't be the hairstylist…"

"Oh, brother," Clint muttered. "Sorry, Mom, but Lila's on a tight schedule. We need to hurry."

"Of course, I understand," Mrs. Landers said, and kept staring like so many awestruck fans.

But Lila didn't mind. For once she was sorry to be a disappointment.

"I know." His mom beamed at them. "How about coming over for dinner? That way we can visit without rushing."

"Nope," Clint said. "She works tonight."

Lila nodded. It was true. But Clint didn't know that.

"It doesn't have to be tonight. What about this weekend?"

"I'd love to," Lila said at the same time Clint said, "No can do."

His mom ignored him and patted Lila's hand. "I'm so looking forward to having you."

15

"YOU NERVOUS?" CLINT SQUEEZED her hand as they lurched over the icy road on their way to his family's ranch.

"No," Lila said. "Yes. But no. Really no. Your mother was as sweet as could be. This is an amazing treat for me." She smiled at him. "What about you? Are you nervous?"

"Damn straight, I am."

She laughed. "Why?"

"You don't know my mom. She's liable to make this into a big to-do. You'd think it's Christmas come early."

"Wow, that'll make the evening even better. Erin thinks I'm nuts around the holidays. I usually start decorating the day after Thanksgiving, and I don't stop singing carols until after New Year's."

"Are you sure that's the only reason she thinks you're nuts?"

"Hey!" Lila let go of his hand so she could punch his arm. "You're really asking for trouble, you know that?"

"Yeah, well…" Clint took her hand in his again. "I knew I was in trouble the moment I met you."

"Huh." She leaned back to look at him. "Should I ask?"

He cleared his throat and muttered, "Probably not."

She sighed, grateful for the ease between them, memorizing the feel of his hand swallowing hers, the slight smile she could see half of, the warmth of the truck against the cold of the wind and the intermittent snow flurries.

When it felt like too much, Lila looked in the small backseat at her bag of treats. Yesterday she'd received her mom's care package filled with all the fixings for their traditional spiced Christmas tea along with some other goodies.

Lila had been delighted at first, but then the truth behind the gesture had sunk in. Her mom had given up hope that Lila could make it home for Christmas. She had to stop thinking about that or she'd be a complete mess.

To make herself feel better, she'd stayed up ungodly late making a big batch of her famous Rocky Road bark, using the microwave in the production trailer.

"I probably should have brought wine," she said.

"Would you stop? When Mom heard you were bringing stuff for your family's traditional tea, she was very excited. Have I mentioned she's more nuts than you about the holidays?"

"She couldn't be."

"Oh, no? Take a look at the gate."

Lila had been so busy staring at Clint she hadn't realized they'd reached the ranch. The gate was large enough for two semitrucks to pass when opened, and it looked like it was made from the pine trees that lined the roads and filled the forests. Hanging at the center was a breathtaking wreath, dotted with holly berries, dusted pinecones and a huge red velvet bow.

"Oh, I think I'm going to fit right in," she said with relief. "And you're sure it's just casual?"

"Lila. You're wearing a skirt, which by itself defies the word casual at our house. Not that I don't appreciate it," he said, eyeing her legs. "A lot."

Grinning, she bumped his shoulder. She hadn't dressed up too much. To go with the pencil skirt she'd chosen a simple cream-colored blouse with a cardigan that was festive but wouldn't be too hot in the kitchen. She'd pulled her hair back in a ponytail, just like she would have if she'd been at home.

"Look, we don't have to stay late. We can be back at the motel by ten if we don't linger over the meal."

"Good grief, we just got here. And lingering is the whole point. That and hearing embarrassing stories about you when you were a kid."

"Fat chance. I've warned everyone to keep their stories to themselves." He put the truck in Park and jumped out to open the big gate. She thought about getting behind the wheel to save him a step, but she wanted to be able to look around.

The long driveway led to a large house at the top of the rise. It was really attractive, a mix of ranch-style and Alpine, with a peaked roof atop the biggest section. And the best part—the whole exterior was decorated to the gills.

Lila took in the lights, the wreath on the door, the garlands around the porch railing and the two big rocking chairs. One thing she didn't have at home was the light dusting of real snow instead of movie-magic Snowcel, which made the whole place look like a gingerbread house. It was magical.

Clint parked the truck next to three others. As she slipped on her jacket, she noticed a barn, a couple of corrals, another big building that was probably a bunk-house, given the smoke coming out of the chimney. The lowing of cattle chased the wind from the valley floor.

Clint carried her bag of goodies as they took the stone walkway to the front door. He touched her lower back, and she glanced at him. "Who were you wav-ing at?" She turned to see, but caught only a glimpse of two cowboys standing outside the barn before Clint blocked her view.

"I wasn't waving," he said in a wry voice. "It's just some of the guys from the bunkhouse. Keep going."

Now, she really wanted to see who he'd flipped off, but the front door swung open before they even reached it.

There was Mr. Landers, it had to be, because he looked like the mold his son was cast from. His salt-and-pepper hair gave her a hint as to what Clint would look like as he got older. Of course he'd be just as striking.

"Welcome, Ms. Loveridge, to our humble home."

"It's Lila, and I'm so happy to be here."

"I'm Doug, Clint's dad, but I reckon you knew that."

Lila grinned. "Well, he does have your good looks."

The older man flushed and laughed.

"There you are," Mrs. Landers said, wiping her hands on a white towel attached to a Santa apron. "Na-than and Beth are already here, and Seth should arrive soon. So come on in, and let's get you two defrosted."

Her jacket was whisked away. The scent of roast beef and fresh rolls made her mouth water. The interior of the house—much more expansive than she'd expected with its high roof and fireplace in the living room—was filled with older, overstuffed chairs, pictures of horses and boys at all stages, trophies and ribbons, studio shots on the walls, and a leather couch that looked as if it had seen a couple of generations grow up.

Another Landers man joined them. He had to be Nathan and the beautiful tall blonde who followed, his wife, Beth. Introductions took less than a minute, they chatted for a few more, then Doug, Nathan and Beth excused themselves because Mrs. Landers had assigned them all *duties*.

Clint seemed pleased that he'd gotten off scot-free so he could show her around. Lila would bet anything he'd be stuck with cleanup. She decided not to burst his bubble as he ushered her into a family room with another fireplace, and a ridiculously perfect Christmas tree standing near a large window. The view was so quintessential it looked like a painted backdrop.

"It's wonderful," she said, taking Clint's hand. Some of the cute Christmas ornaments looked handmade. "Better than I even imagined."

"The house was originally built by my great-grandfather," he said, "then extended by my grandad and Dad. It's a real ranch home with enough room to house half a dozen hands, and enough supplies to last a Montana winter."

"Well, I can see it's a real hardship for you to live here."

He leaned in and surprised her with a kiss on the lips. Without even looking to see if anyone was watching. He kept it brief and G-rated, which was more than fine with her. Even so she sneaked a peek behind them.

He smiled and nodded at the window. "It's getting dark, but you can still see we have a great view of the Rockies."

"The house you want to build, would it be near

here?" she asked and saw him stiffen. "I'm sorry. Maybe I shouldn't—I won't bring it up again."

"No," he said, shrugging. "It's fine." He turned back to the window. "It's not a secret. I'm just having trouble deciding between two spots, but yeah, it'll be about a mile or so north."

"Darn, I wish we had more daylight."

"I can always bring you back out..." He met her gaze. "If you have time."

Something was making her tongue stick. Looking into his eyes often made her heart flutter. But this was different...

"Come on," he said with a small resigned smile that she hoped was her imagination. "I'll show you my mother's pride and joy."

A few more surprises met her in the kitchen. Double ovens and a six-burner stove, an island big enough for four people to work at. Laughter floated in from another room. This house, the holiday songs coming from the family room, the scents, the décor, it was all a bit overwhelming.

She had to blink back tears as she thought of her family's much smaller home in LA where her mom and dad and Brit had the tree up. Her brother was married and had his own home, but he and Cheryl lived close and would spend Christmas at the house.

"Hey," Clint said, his big hand landing softly on her shoulder. "You okay?"

"Just missing my family."

"I wish there was something I could have done about that."

"You have. Believe me. I'm fine."

"Then get in there and make that spiced tea you told

me about. I want to try it. I'm sure my mom will be back in a second."

"Yes, sir," she said, taking the bag with her to the island. First thing she brought out was the Rocky Road bark, made with semisweet chocolate, mini-marshmallows, slivered almonds and little pieces of peppermint stick and toffee. The *tray* was just a cookie sheet covered with tinfoil, but she hadn't had much to work with.

As soon as she uncovered it, Mrs. Landers, who insisted Lila call her Meryl, joined her at the island. "Oh, my. Doesn't that look sinfully delicious?"

Coming up behind Clint's mom, Beth let out a moan that made Lila blush. "What's this called? Better than Sex?"

"Oh, Beth." Laughing, Meryl swatted at her daughter-in-law as she reached for a piece.

Beth took a bite. "Oh, yeah," she murmured, eyes closed.

They all laughed, and it helped Lila relax. The three men flowed through the kitchen, snatching pieces of her bark as they got water and wine glasses to put on the dining-room table.

Clint's grandmother, fresh from a nap, appeared and was introduced. Tall and lean like her son and grandsons, she looked to be in her eighties, with wrinkles that showed the rancher's life she'd lived, her silver hair tied up in a high swirl.

"Here, honey," Meryl said, handing Lila an apron with a snowman on the front. "We don't want that pretty sweater ruined."

Most of the meal was either ready or baking in the oven. A couple dishes needed tending, and there were always last-minute details. All in all, Meryl was so organized she didn't even use a cheat sheet.

While she brought out serving bowls from the cabinets, Clint's grandmother, Shirley, sampled the Rocky Road. "I think I'm going to have to hide this bark you brought, or the men will all be stuffed before supper."

"Where are you going to hide it, Grandma?" Beth asked sweetly as she plucked a holiday apron from the drawer. "Your room?" She met the older woman's squinty gaze and burst out laughing.

"You hush up, Beth Landers," Grandma Landers said, holding up a wooden spoon.

Lila couldn't help but laugh. They were all wonderful. She could tell Clint's family all genuinely liked one another. She could hear the three men talking and laughing in the family room. And Nathan and Beth, they'd been married only a year, yet Beth already belonged.

A few minutes later, as Lila finished sautéing some fresh green beans, she caught Clint at the edge of the kitchen door. He didn't say anything; he was just checking on her, she was sure. She tried not to let him know she'd seen him, but it was impossible not to smile. He was the very best part of her life these days.

After all the crap that was going on with Baxter and Jason and her own feelings of disillusionment about show business, it was crazy how much she needed him at the end of the day. At first it had just been fun and exciting. He was so hot, yet funny and kind, a rare combination in a man. And her feelings had changed; she'd known that since the barbecue. But there simply wasn't anything to do about it. He belonged here with his family, on Landers land.

As for her, well, Lila didn't know where she belonged anymore. If it weren't for Erin, sometimes Lila swore she would just quit, walk away, pretend the twenty-year-old dream had never existed. The thought was scary, but also liberating. And that only made it twice as scary.

No matter what, though, she would remember Clint, his family and this dinner. It couldn't have come at a more perfect time for her.

The three women laughed about something, snapping her out of her gloomy thoughts.

Evidently Beth, who was working on a carrot-and-raisin salad, had told a story about Nathan and her niece Liberty. Lila was sorry she missed it. She promised herself she'd stay present, as she put together the special Spiced Christmas Tea made with star anise, cinnamon and passion fruit nectar.

"One Christmas," Meryl said, as she checked on the dinner rolls, "Clint found a dog out by the gate. A rangy looking, big old mutt who was shivering in the cold and absolutely covered in mud. Well, that boy could never turn away an animal in need, so he snuck that dog in, trying to keep him quiet in the mudroom so we'd be none the wiser. Of course he had to show his brothers. You can guess what happened.

"The dog got out, went straight for the big turkey that had been resting on the counter, took it down and went to town. When the boys tried to get the turkey back, the dog made a run for it, pretty much destroying half the dinner table and most of the presents under the tree."

"What did you do?"

"Ate cold cuts and whatever we could salvage, tied the dog up in the barn, and the boys spent most of their evening cleaning up the mess."

When she finished laughing, Lila said, "My mother could tell you a few juicy stories about my brother."

"It's just the two of you?"

"I have a sister, too. But Brit and I were angels." Lila barely got the lie out without laughing.

The other three joined in and she couldn't have felt more at home.

BY THE TIME they were all seated around the table, one empty chair for Seth, should he decide to show up, Clint was slightly buzzed from a glass of his father's best whiskey. He'd felt a little guilty about leaving Lila on her own in the kitchen, but he'd sneaked by a few times to check on her, and she'd been laughing and cooking and making herself at home.

She looked really happy. As happy as he'd seen her. It was like there were two Lilas—the actress who looked so delicate and beautiful she seemed like a different kind of human, but who would show up in purple hair or with crazy eye makeup, all business in the trailer, and putting up with the rowdy crew; and then there was this Lila, who looked as if she belonged in a home filled with family, a life of simple pleasures and down-to-earth dreams.

Funny enough, he liked both of them. All of her quirks and her mischief, especially when that wicked streak showed up in bed.

She sat between him and Beth, and those two hit it off like gangbusters. What did surprise him was that tiny Lila could eat like one of the ranch hands. Usually she stuck to salads. Tonight she had double helpings.

"Meryl tells me you're an actress," Grandma Landers said from across the table. "Nathan's first wife, Anne, she was an actress, too. Pity about the accident. She was a sweet girl. Had a real nice touch growing roses."

Clint's gaze went straight to Nathan, who was letting go of a deep breath, then to Lila. She'd obviously picked up the sudden tension around the table. Even his parents had. His grandmother hadn't meant anything by her comment, but with Beth there, the topic was tricky.

Though, Beth looked perfectly fine.

"I'm not acting in this film, Mrs. Landers. I'm part of the crew. I do hair and makeup."

"I've never been much for the movies," she said. "I like a few TV shows though. That Ellen DeGeneres. She's funny. And she doesn't curse like so many young people do."

"You're right," Lila said, "she is funny."

"Have you ever met her? I think she lives in Hollywood."

Lila smiled. "No. I haven't. But I know people who have, and they say she's very nice."

Clint relaxed. As he finished his second helping of mashed potatoes and gravy, he realized something. He'd been a little worried about tonight, but it had nothing to do with Lila not fitting in as he'd thought. Now he understood that wasn't the issue at all. Of course she fit in. He'd already seen how she acted in town, at the motel, with other members of the crew.

The real issue was that he'd already started picturing her in the house he was going to build. And that was a mistake he couldn't afford to make.

A rush of cold air hit the back of his neck, and everyone turned to the sound of feet stomping on the front door mat. Seth had made it after all. Clint hadn't thought he would. Of course he was late.

"Hello everybody," he said, sweeping off his snowy Stetson, spraying water over the floor. "It smells good in here. And I'm starving."

Their mom was up like a shot, pulling him into her

arms as if she hadn't seen him in years. Which was fine. Better to keep welcoming him home. Maybe it would stick at some point. Make him forget about whatever the hell he'd been running down to Billings for and re-acquaint himself with the family. Nathan and Clint exchanged looks, but tonight wasn't the time to get into any heavy discussions.

"He looks just like you and Nathan," Lila whispered as she leaned close to Clint.

He breathed in her seductive scent and almost didn't see Seth's jaw drop when he noticed Lila. Clint hid a smile. Sure would've been a pity to miss that. They weren't competitive, not when it came to women. Sports, definitely.

"Hey, Seth." Clint rested his arm on the back of her chair. "This is Lila." To her, he said, "Seth's our baby brother."

Shaking his head, Seth snorted a laugh. He came around the table and shook her hand. "Lila, nice to meet you. What are you doing slumming it with this guy?"

"All right, boys." Meryl pulled out Seth's chair. "That's enough."

"Boys?" Clint frowned. He and Nathan looked at each other. "We didn't say anything."

"Baby brother?" Seth kissed their mom's cheek before he sat. "Nah. You weren't trying to bait me."

"What? Is that not a true statement?" Clint felt Lila's gentle touch on his thigh. "Okay. Truce."

"Fine. Truce," Seth muttered, and then laughed.

So did Nathan and Clint.

"Okay," their mom said, "Seth, I'll warm a plate for you. As for everybody else, you all better have saved room for dessert. I made my blue ribbon deep-dish apple pie and pumpkin chiffon."

"Which took second place two years running," Seth added as he got to his feet.

"Where are you going? You just got here."

Seeing the worry on his mom's face made Clint's chest tighten. He was a second away from telling Seth to shove the truce.

"I can warm my own plate, Mom," Seth said in a low voice. "I should've been on time. You go take care of dessert."

Clint glanced at his father who hadn't said one word since Seth had arrived.

Lila moaned. "I've eaten your weight in food already. And you know I can't resist pie."

Clint slid his arm from the back of her chair and draped it around her shoulders. He knew she was trying to be a buffer. "Of course you can't."

"It's only polite to have a piece of both."

He nodded.

"Does she serve them with ice cream?"

"How are you so small?" he said, laughing at the seriousness of her tone.

"Please, you know I live on salads most of the time. Which gets very old. I sure won't miss that."

The odd comment caught him off guard. "What do you mean?"

Lila blinked. "Nothing. I just— Nothing." She smiled and turned to Beth.

Nothing?

Like hell.

16

"I HAD A wonderful time." Feeling pleasantly tired, Lila settled in the truck's comfy seat.

"I'm glad you enjoyed yourself," he said. "Everyone thought you were great."

She wished there wasn't the console between them, when all she wanted was to snuggle up against him. But she made do with his hand in hers.

"Your mom's pies are amazing. I can't believe she gave me a slice of each. I really hope I don't eat them both tonight."

Clint lifted a brow at her. "You're serious."

She just laughed, then remembered her earlier remark about salads getting old. How utterly thoughtless. She'd have to be more careful and not give anyone the wrong idea.

It wasn't that she didn't trust Clint. She hadn't told anyone, not even Erin, God, especially not Erin. They'd made a pact to conquer Hollywood or die trying. They were in this stupid business for the long haul.

Lila couldn't really explain to anyone that she'd lost her enthusiasm because she didn't understand it herself yet. Of course being stuck on location for eternity had something to do with it. Plus it was the holidays, and she missed her family. If she could just make it past Christmas, maybe all the doubt would go away and she'd be back to her normal self.

"Tell me about Seth," she said. "How much younger is he than you?"

"Two years. But he acts like he's twelve."

Lila bit her lip. Clint hadn't exactly been the paragon of maturity when it came to baiting Seth.

"He got into a little trouble in college, nothing big, he moved past it. Then a year after he graduated he joined the air force. Not a single word to any of us. Told us the day before he shipped out. It about killed my mom."

"Well, obviously he isn't career military."

"No, he came home after four years."

"So he works the ranch with you?"

"Sort of…when he feels like it. He'd lived in Billings for a while and keeps running back there. He's kept himself away from the family for the most part. We're not sure what's going on with him. We've all tried talking to him, but he's not saying."

"Can't be easy for him," Lila said, laying her head back.

"Easy?" Clint gave her a sharp look. "What do you mean?"

"He's got some big shoes to fill, given how amazing you and Nathan are. I'm sure that's got to put on some pressure."

"No, Seth is smart. He was one of those kids who didn't have to study and still got better grades than Nathan and me."

"Yeah, but you guys are ranchers. I mean, how important was it to—You know what? I have no idea what

I'm talking about. I know nothing about ranchers or their mind-set or anything else."

"Maybe not," he said. "But humor me. Finish what you were going to say."

"Look, I just met your family. I feel like a dope making any kind of observation."

"An objective one is usually the best."

Lila sighed. "You and Nathan seem to be more like your dad. The ranch, the land, you take pride in the work and preserving your home for future generations." She brought her head up. "And before you get the wrong idea, I'm not saying Seth doesn't feel that way, too. Obviously I don't even know him. But coming up behind two older brothers who are making your dad and the Landers name proud...

"Well, it's got to be tough. I'm guessing grades didn't matter all that much to any of you. And of course I could be...full of beans." Lila laughed softly, hoping she hadn't offended Clint. He looked so solemn. "I hadn't even heard that phrase before coming to Montana, can you believe that?"

Clint didn't answer.

Feeling she'd overstepped and desperate to fill the silence, she couldn't think of anything to say but, "I'm sorry."

"Don't be. I'm just thinking about what you said. Seth and I had always been close, and you might have a point. I just wish I knew how to get him to open up about it."

"I have a feeling, just watching him tonight, that he misses you all. That's a start."

"I hope so. For my mom's sake." Clint smiled. "For all our sakes. What about you?" he said. "Whose expectations are you trying to meet?"

"Erin's," she said without even thinking. He probably thought she was joking. And that she had a lot of nerve dodging his question after psychoanalyzing his family. Lila sighed. "Erin's parents worked long hours, and she practically lived at our house when we were kids. She's as much a sister to me as Brit. Maybe even more, and yes, I feel horribly guilty saying that. But it's the truth. We used to be inseparable. Since she met Spencer, things have changed, so you're not getting a good picture of how close we used to be."

"I bet you're still close."

"Yes, of course, we are. Definitely. It's just that… it might sound stupid, but I really don't want to disappoint her. We've shared the same dream for twenty years." Lila felt disloyal and sad just speaking the words. "Hypothetically, because I'm not saying I want to quit, okay? I'm not. I'm just trying to answer your question. So, hypothetically, if I decided I wanted out, I would feel as if I was betraying Erin."

Clint didn't speak for about a minute. Then all he said was, "Damn."

"Yeah," Lila said, sighing. "And my parents. They've always been supportive, never once discouraged me from studying drama. They paid for my entire tuition for UCLA because they believe in me." She felt her throat tighten. She'd said too much. What was wrong with her? They'd had such a nice evening, and she was ruining everything. She forced a laugh. "I have no idea how we ended up here. I'm sorry I made this about me. Because those aren't even real issues." She paused, grasping for something else to talk about. "Why don't you tell me more about Anne? You never mentioned knowing someone in the business."

Another long silence had her feeling prickly. Did

it have to do with what she'd just told him? Or was it about Anne?

"Don't be sorry," he said finally. "I know you were trying to make me feel better about the whole Seth situation."

Whether he really believed that, she had no way of knowing, but she was grateful just to be able to breathe again.

"Anne died a few years after they were married," Clint said, and Lila winced. "Every time Nathan was out of town on business, she'd go to Kalispell or wherever the regional theater was holding auditions. She was my age, we were in school together and she loved drama class. But she'd never said anything about wanting to be an actress. According to her friend Bella, Anne had obsessed over whether she could've made it big. Nathan felt as if he hadn't known her at all. For a while, he was a wreck. Three years later he met Beth, and she turned his world right again."

"Oh, that's so sad about Anne. No wonder it got so quiet."

Clint nodded. "I have a feeling he knows everything there is to know about Beth."

"I'm sure," she said, wondering how many people at that dinner table were thinking about her being an actress. Someone who would always be chasing her dream no matter what the cost. A woman who wasn't right for Clint. Just another reason they were location lovers and nothing more.

She looked out the passenger window, her mood plummeting. She'd always tried to be honest with herself. She'd loved being with Clint tonight. With his family. It was all too easy to picture herself in his world.

Lila wanted kids. Even Erin didn't know that because Lila couldn't tell her. An actress looking for her big break didn't commit career suicide by starting a family. So, yes, they were close, and yet they weren't. Not if Lila wanted to keep a dream alive that she was no longer sure she wanted.

And then here was Clint. Gorgeous, kind, dependable, perfect.

Temporary.

Lila could just cry.

BY THE TIME they reached the motel, Lila had promised herself she wouldn't be a buzzkill. She was going to make the most of their time left together. Tonight. Every night. Every minute they could be together.

She had her jacket off before the door closed. She tossed it, wound her arms around Clint's neck and kissed him hard. She knew she'd surprised him, but he responded quickly.

He pulled her close and teased the seam of her lips until she opened them for him. His tongue swept inside her mouth. She tasted the faint sweetness of his mother's apple pie. Lila met each slow stroke of his tongue with a caress of her own and pressed closer.

Breaking the kiss, he leaned back to look at her. His dark eyes searched her face as his mouth curved in a warm smile. Was he for real?

It would be so much simpler if he weren't. She'd been asking herself that question since the barbecue. They'd met just over two weeks ago, and it was hard to separate reality from what she wanted to believe. She knew the answer. Even before tonight.

"It's okay. I know you can't stay." She'd lied. It wasn't okay at all.

"Why is that?"

"Your parents and grandmother…" She didn't understand his bewildered expression. "They'll know where you were…"

Clint smiled and slowly moved his hands up and down her back. The repetitive motion felt incredibly soothing.

"I guess we can set the alarm," she murmured, wanting to close her eyes and just feel his hands while she daydreamed.

He raised his eyebrows in question.

"In case we fall asleep."

His hands stopped at the top of her backside. "Do you have to work tonight?" he asked, frowning. "Or does this have to do with my *curfew*?"

Lila sighed. "I didn't say that."

"Listen, I hate that I'm still living with my folks, and I'd never rub anything in their faces. But I'm sure as hell not going to let them interfere with my private life."

"I understand." Lila lowered her arms from around his neck. When he didn't release her, she rested her hands on his biceps. "The thing is, I really don't want them to think poorly of me."

Comprehension dawned in his face. Briefly. And then the frown was back.

"I know it doesn't matter. They don't consider me…" She drew in a breath. What? A good prospect? Appropriate for Clint? True or not, she couldn't say that out loud.

"Consider you what?"

She hesitated. "Please don't make me say it."

"Is this about Anne?"

"No." She understood that might also be a problem. "Yes. Partly. My lifestyle is…unpredictable. Although, I do have that role in the sequel." So it wasn't as if she was chasing an illusive dream. Her hard work was about to pay off. But she knew far too many people like Anne. Always certain their big chance was around the corner. Clearing her throat, she shrugged. "I mean, they know I'm leaving soon, right?"

Clint tensed. His face. His whole body. Then he relaxed and nodded. "They do."

Lila sighed. "Well, I sure know how to ruin a party." She tried to step back, but he held her tighter.

"It's just beginning," he said with a thoroughly wicked smile as he backed her toward the bed.

Relieved, she lifted her arms to put them around his neck. He stopped her and gently pushed her sweater off her shoulders.

"Okay," she muttered, and caught the edges of his shirtfront and yanked. All but one snap popped.

Clint laughed. "Okay, so we're taking off the gloves."

"And everything else." She slid her palms up his strong chest. God, he felt so good. She touched the tip of her tongue to his flat dark nipple.

He jerked, grunted.

"Wow, sensitive tonight."

Before she could get to the second one, he started unbuttoning her blouse. Slowly, with the utmost care. Probably worried his callused fingers would snag the delicate fabric.

After he'd set the sweater and blouse aside, he picked her up and laid her on the bed. Getting settled, she accidentally kicked out a foot, making Clint jump back.

"Oops. Sorry," she said. "Good thing you're fast."

"Now that might've ruined the party."

She unfastened her skirt. "Can't have that."

He just stood there looking at her with an odd smile on his face.

"May I help you?" she asked, narrowing her eyes.

"The whole time we were eating supper I wondered which bra you were wearing."

She glanced down at the cream satin demi-cups. "And do you approve?"

He flicked the front clasp and bared her breasts. "I do now," he said, and bent to take a nipple into his mouth. He sucked hard and did something amazing with his tongue.

Warmth spread from her chest to her belly to the dampness between her thighs. She lifted her shoulders off the mattress, enough to reach his ear. She bit his lobe and felt him smile against her breast.

Then he took a slight nip.

"Ouch!"

"That didn't hurt," he murmured, taking a long slow swipe with his tongue.

"It surprised me." She arched her back. "Do it again."

He straightened and removed his shirt. "And have you think I'm a one-trick pony?"

"That particular trick stays in your repertoire. Got it?"

As he unfastened his jeans, he raked a gaze across her breasts.

"You've seen them before," she said, a giggle bubbling at the back of her throat when his mouth quirked up only on one side. That meant she was in for something naughty. Something she was going to like a whole lot.

After unzipping his fly, he sat on the edge of the bed. Keeping an eye on her, he removed the first boot.

She didn't like that he hadn't said anything. She got up on her knees, let the bra slide off, and pressed her breasts against his back and nibbled his neck.

His body jerked, and he laughed.

"Ah...you're ticklish?" She started in the middle of his shoulder so she could get some build-up going. Her lips barely grazed his skin.

"Lila?"

"Clint."

"Listen to me."

"Uh-huh." She bit down.

He had her on her back, pressed into the mattress, restraining her with a palm against her ribs before she could react. With his free hand he tried to peel her skirt over her hips.

"Lift," he ordered.

"Take your jeans off first." The words came out jumbled. She was laughing and hadn't caught her breath from his sly move.

He released her, and feeling triumphant, she got up on her elbows to watch him strip.

His hand shot out. It locked around her ankle, and she gasped. Her left elbow gave out, and she fell back. He grabbed her other ankle and hauled her to the edge of the bed.

She should've known better. So much for enjoying her moment of victory.

Clint didn't tell her to lift her butt again. He managed just fine, stripping off her skirt and her thong. And then stood there like a conquering pirate surveying his spoils while he shoved his own jeans off.

Still wearing his boxers, he spread her legs and stroked the skin of her inner thigh. A slight shiver passed through her. When he dropped to a crouch, she held her breath.

"You're not laughing," he said with a cocky grin, and kissed the sensitive flesh close to her sex.

She'd never felt more vulnerable, more exposed in her life. Swallowing, she lifted her chin. "Never figured you for a sore loser."

"I'm the loser?"

"Who's going down on whom?"

He let out a loud laugh. "Good point," he muttered, still laughing when he pressed his mouth against her core.

Holy crap!

The slight vibration of his lips felt amazing. She squirmed, causing him to look up. "Don't stop."

His mouth was damp, his eyes darker than a moonless night. "I win either way," he said with a sexy smile.

"Me, too. Please, feel free to go to town."

Again he covered her with his mouth and used his tongue to make her squirm. And yowzah, did it feel good.

Lying back, she gasped and writhed. And clutched at his hair at the first signs of a climax. But she didn't want to come yet. She moved back, and managed a quick trick reversal of her own so that she was in a position to take him in her mouth.

He groaned and almost jackknifed when she sucked especially hard.

She glanced up. "Was that a good groan or an ouch groan?"

"It was too good." He pulled her upright and kissed her hard. His tongue chased hers, stroked it, flicked it, then thrust in and out, mimicking everything he'd already done and would do again soon.

Finally they both gasped for air.

"If you're looking for my tonsils, I had them out at seven," she said, barely able to breathe. Laughing didn't help. "Hey." She saw him rolling on a condom. He'd worked fast.

"What?"

"I wasn't finished."

"I'm not either." He picked her up and moved her to center stage. "Two or three pillows?"

"Depends. Where are you putting them?"

Leaning over her, he licked her left breast and tucked a second pillow behind her head. He stacked two under her butt.

Lila grinned. "I'm going to like this, huh?"

Clint's eyes were intense. He was on a mission. He spread her thighs wider and got between them. Before she could take her next breath, he'd found her clit and rubbed it with his thumb.

"Oh," she said with a soft gasp. A jolt of electricity shot up her spine. "You might want to wait on that."

He kissed one breast, then sucked the other.

His thumb increased the pressure.

"Uh, Clint."

"Yes, sweetheart?"

"Clint," she practically yelled and arched off the mattress. "I'm not kidding."

He stroked the hair away from her face and kissed her neck. And then he whispered, "Neither am I."

He entered her, driving in quick and deep, still thumbing her clit. Oh, God, he really had to stop. She drew in the musky male scent of his skin and moaned.

Everything happened at once. The shooting stars behind her eyelids. The fevered rush of pleasure, so familiar, yet new and different. She writhed and begged, and he wouldn't let up.

She started to calm down just as he withdrew. He pulled her legs tightly around his hips and plunged inside her again, then kept moving back and forth, picking up speed, plunging deeper. She liked the angle; he was hitting lots of sensitive places. But he stopped.

Her protest was cut short when he put her legs over his shoulders. He rocked gently against her. "How's this? Okay?"

Panting, she just nodded.

Holding her gaze, Clint leaned down. His eyes were so dark, even this close she couldn't make out the pupils. "I should punish you for wearing that skirt tonight," he said, his voice a hoarse whisper.

"I thought you liked it."

"Your legs are indecently long and very hot." He pushed in farther, and she clutched the sheet.

"So what's the problem?"

"I had to sit through dinner, across the table from my parents, harder than a rock thanks to that damn skirt."

"Well, I'm glad I had nothing to do with it."

A faint smile curved his mouth. He leaned close enough their lips touched, and embedded himself so deep inside her it left her breathless.

She managed a weak whimper. "Please."

Clint pressed his lips against hers. The angle and pressure hit a hot spot that set her insides on fire. He started thrusting and pumping, his face taut, eyes locked with hers. She dug her fingers into his shoulder muscles, clinging to him, as her body roared toward a second release.

They climaxed together, both moaning and murmuring incoherent words. Her hands slid from his sweat-slick skin.

Slowly he moved one leg off his shoulder, kissing the inside of her ankle before lifting her other leg and letting it down.

Clint collapsed beside her, falling hard, as if he had no energy left. Then he pulled her into his arms and cradled her with his body, keeping her close, safe and warm.

17

AFTER WASHING HER brushes and tidying up, Lila stepped out of the trailer and looked up at the overcast sky. Three days ago the news channels had predicted snow for most of the week. So far they'd only had passing flurries, which turned out well for the crew and shooting schedule in general.

For Lila, the shorter days meant she had more time for Clint. They hadn't needed him on the set, so she didn't get to see him until after work. But since dinner with his family, he'd spent every night with her. Lila wasn't sure how she'd feel about running into his mom again. She'd probably blush to high heaven.

She scanned the groups of crew and extras, hoping to spot Erin. They still hadn't talked, though not for lack of Lila trying. Erin had become wily about disappearing the minute they wrapped each day. Lila was beginning to think she should ask Clint for a ride to Shadow Creek so she could corner Erin.

Finally Lila saw Erin conferring with the new camera assistant. They were between scenes, so Lila grabbed a jacket and hurried toward them, hoping to pull Erin aside the second they were finished. The borrowed jacket was big, but Lila wrapped it snugly around her body and pulled up the collar. Just because no snow had fallen didn't mean she wasn't freezing her butt off.

Yeah, so much for her big, fat, glamorous Hollywood life.

Too late she saw Jason approaching Erin from the other side.

He reached her first and barged right into the conversation. "What do you think, Erin? Were you happy with that last take? I'm not sure I was feeling it."

She glanced at him, and without answering, returned her attention to the young assistant. The poor guy shifted nervously. First rule on any set, don't piss off the director.

Lila hung back and imagined the steam coming out of Jason's ears. To say he was pissed would be putting it mildly. He folded his arms across his chest and glared at Erin's back. But he didn't say a word.

It wasn't unusual for him and Erin to get into disagreements. They'd been crossing swords since college. But they rarely argued in public. That was, until a few weeks ago.

Knowing Erin and the terrible mood she'd been in, Lila figured she'd keep talking and make Jason wait. Since Lila wasn't about to get in the middle of their feud and he hadn't noticed her yet, she decided she'd catch Erin later.

She slowly swiveled around and made it a few feet.

"Hey, Blondie."

Cringing, she stopped, counted to five and turned to face Jason's silly frat boy grin. "Do you really want to dig out the old nicknames? Let's see, what was yours? I'm sure it'll come to me."

"The grouch must be rubbing off on you," he muttered, glancing at Erin.

"Huh." Lila paused, then moved closer so no one could overhear, even though he didn't deserve the courtesy. "No, it's you. Annoying Erin and me." And most of the crew, but she wouldn't speak for them.

Jason spread his hands. "What did I do to you?"

Interesting. He hadn't included Erin.

"Your lack of communication is unprofessional and rude, for one thing." She waited for the denial, but he just shook his head. "How many people have the final revision?"

He didn't answer, and Lila was fine with stretching out the silence. Hopefully it would make him uncomfortable. Sure, he was under a lot of pressure and worried about the weather. She even sympathized...to some degree.

Erin walked up, looking Jason straight in the eye. "Don't ever interrupt me like that again." Just as she turned to Lila, as though it was an afterthought, Erin added, "The take was fine. Come on, Lila. What is it you need? We'll have to walk and talk. I'm late."

Lila caught a glimpse of anger in Jason's face before she fell into step beside Erin. Her stomach rebelled. She hadn't seen them interact for a while, and the animosity between them was worse than she suspected. Erin didn't hold grudges. She might not agree with something, but she always kept a tight lid on her emotions for the sake of the work.

"What are you late for?"

"Nothing." Erin glanced at her phone. "I just didn't want to talk to him."

"Can you sneak in a break?" Lila asked casually.

"Sure." Erin blinked and slowed down a step. Probably figured out what was coming. "I only have a few minutes, though."

"Baloney. We need to talk, and we're doing it right now."

"Come on, Lila. I'm working. You know this isn't the time or place."

"You've been avoiding me, and you haven't told me anything about what's going on. So no, actually, I have no idea if this is the time or place."

"Look, we'll talk. Later." Erin stopped when Lila did, and they faced each other. "This evening. I promise."

"You'll disappear on me." Lila felt the sting of tears. She blinked them back and held firm. "Now."

Erin's snorted. "Turn off the waterworks. I don't need you playing me, too."

Lila could barely breathe. Shocked and hurt to the bone, she stared at her friend. After several long seconds, afraid she couldn't hold back the tears, Lila turned and walked away.

"Wait. Please, wait." Erin caught up with her. "Dammit. I'm sorry, Lila. I didn't mean it. Jesus. I'm such a shithead."

"Yes, you are," Lila muttered and kept walking, anger overtaking hurt.

"I'm sorry. I really am. You're the last person on earth I'd want to hurt."

Three weeks ago Lila would've believed it. She walked faster, her much longer legs making it hard for Erin to keep up.

"Okay, we'll talk." Erin jogged a few steps ahead and swung around to face her, walking backward. "Right now. Wherever you want. I'll explain everything. God, I'm so sorry," she said, her voice cracking. "Please believe that, if nothing else."

Lila stopped and looked at her friend's stricken expression. Tears glistened in Erin's eyes. She'd cried maybe twice in the twenty years they'd known each other. But it was the crack in her voice that had gotten to Lila.

"I don't have an excuse," Erin said. "I've been horrible, I know, and I—"

"You don't need an excuse. We're friends. You're allowed. I'm sorry, too." Lila swallowed back a lump of tears. "But if you don't follow me to the trailer right this minute and spill everything, I'm going to tell Baxter you have a huge crush on him."

"Huh." Erin sniffed. "I turn my back for a couple weeks and you morph into this evil being."

"Couple weeks, my foot." Lila turned around and resumed her breakneck pace.

Erin sighed and followed.

Ignoring the stares, neither of them spoke until they were inside the hair-and-makeup trailer with the door locked.

Lila sank onto a chair. "Remember, you said everything."

Rubbing her eyes, Erin nodded. She lowered her hands. "Baxter is going to be the first AD for the sequel."

A startled laugh escaped Lila. "Come on…don't waste time joking."

"I wish I were joking. I really do."

"How is that possible? He's an idiot!"

"I'm pretty sure the whole crew and cast agrees with that." Erin exhaled harshly. "His uncle wrote a large check."

"Jason promised you that position and not just because he owes you. You know the job better than anyone, and you've worked harder than anybody else. How many months did you spend scouting locations, living on junk food because there's no per diem money in the budget—"

"It's okay, Lila. Yes, I'm upset, disappointed, all those things. But Jason did what he thought was best for the project. We can't understand what kind of pressure a director is under. In his shoes I might've done the same thing."

"Oh, please. I don't believe that, and neither do you. We've always hated the Hollywood double-talk, the empty promises, using people... You would never have done that to Jason, or any of us."

"You're probably right."

"No probably about it," Lila muttered. "I'm so mad at him."

"See, that's why I didn't want to tell you. Your role is safe. You'll be playing Tara. Don't do anything to mess that up."

"How can you say that? Nothing's sacred. Jason just proved we can't trust him." Lila closed her eyes for a second. "You know, even though he's been short-tempered and annoying, I still believed in him. I wanted him to succeed. He's worked hard since college."

"I *still* believe in him."

"How can you, Erin? Why would you even stick around? Jason needs you. Let him flounder and see just how much."

She turned away.

Lila frowned. "Baxter has no idea what he's doing. The sequel is going to end up a complete mess." She stared at her friend's back. "Erin? What else? You promised."

She cleared her throat and turned around. "Unofficially I'll be the first AD. I'll be paid a salary and everything—"

"And Baxter gets the credit."

Erin nodded.

"You don't care about the money, it was always about the credits for the Director's Guild. What's Baxter going to do with them? Nobody's ever going to hire him to do a film."

"Look on the bright side." Erin smiled. "I'll be making sure our investment pays off. We can get rid of our loans."

Lila stared at her hands. She was almost glad when Erin's phone signaled a text. They probably needed her back on the set, and Lila could use some alone time. How could Erin not be furious and hurt? How could she think Lila wouldn't be, as well? If Jason screwed Erin, then he screwed Lila, too. She didn't even want the role anymore.

"Yep, gotta go," Erin said, looking up from her phone. "Actually I'm glad I finally told you. I've been nasty to Jason, and it's not really fair since I agreed to the deal. We'll all benefit in the end."

Lila forced a smile. It was the best she could do, considering her friend had sold her soul to the devil.

IT HAD BEEN another long frustrating day on the set, and while Lila had avoided most everyone she didn't want to see, she'd had two encounters with Baxter that made her want to FedEx him to Iceland. In his tighty-whities.

At last, though, she was in the right place with the exact right person.

Clint had met her at the motel just after eight, taken one look at her and started running a bath in her heavenly hotel room. He'd gone to pick up food from the diner while she'd soaked and let some of the tension ease from her body.

She'd never been with a man who'd been that considerate without it being about sex. Ever. He'd just been kind, that's all, and here she was, in the throes, as they say, of a very big dilemma.

What she'd like very much to do was lay it all out for him, piece by piece, but since she wasn't sure that any of the pieces made sense, she didn't think it was time. Or maybe it wasn't appropriate. Probably both.

He wouldn't understand, anyway. She'd end up sounding like a Tinseltown flake, which was the last thing she wanted. If she'd really wanted to be fair, she'd tell him they should skip tonight, make plans for tomorrow. But since she'd worked for fifteen hours yesterday, they'd only talked on the phone, and she wasn't willing to do it again.

Not when there were so few nights ahead of them. Maybe if they ate and made love, her mind would just shut off and she wouldn't have to think about how badly she wanted to quit. Walk away. She still hadn't come to terms with Erin's willingness to continue working with Jason.

That backstabbing wiener. How many times had Erin saved his hide on this film? On every project they'd ever worked on, but especially this one. The one that counted. And how did he repay her? By giving her job to a butt-head.

Just thinking about it made her muscles tense—and just when she'd finally loosened up.

Hearing the door to the outer room open, she smiled, ready to get out of the tub and into bed with Clint. She quickly dried off, and just as he knocked, she wrapped the towel around herself. "I'll be right there."

"Take your time. I got the rotisserie chicken you like, and a salad with Italian on the side."

"Sounds great. What did you get?" She wiped off the mirror with her hand, but wished she hadn't when she saw how she looked. Her hair was still in a ponytail, but her eye makeup was smudged, her complexion spotty and she looked about a hundred years old.

But since Clint seemed to like her anyway, she exited the bathroom without giving it another thought.

He'd made the room perfect. The pillows were pushed up against the headboard, the covers turned down, their dinners were laid out on flattened paper bags, complete with a cold beer on each bedside table.

"I got a burger," Clint said, sounding like a manly man. "With cheese and fries."

"Mmm. Sounds yummy. You won't mind if I dine au naturel, will you?" she said, tossing away the bath towel.

He just sputtered in response.

Once she climbed in bed, she pulled the covers up under her arms and watched him strip. Definitely the highlight of her day...so far, anyway.

He uncapped the beers, then joined her. The eating was pretty silent. They both were famished, and as the hunger started to settle, her tangled thoughts took over.

The thing was, quitting was a huge decision. Of course she'd stay until this film wrapped because she'd given her word, but after that? Could she really work with Jason again? And Baxter?

God, the idea was horrible. But bowing out meant leaving Erin on her own, and that would be equally horrible. Plus there was something else to consider. Was she just using what happened to Erin as an excuse for something she hadn't had the guts to do on her own? Spending three months working on location had really opened her eyes. Made her reevaluate what she wanted her life to look like in ten years.

Erin wouldn't understand at first; the role of Tara was too major to give up. She'd advise Lila to suck it up, grab the credit, and after the sequel was finished, Lila wouldn't have to ever work with Jason again.

A very good argument. If Lila still cared about acting.

Honestly? A role like Tara was only going to add to the pressure she already felt. It was such a cutthroat profession, and there was always going to be someone prettier, younger, more connected.

Clint put his beer bottle down loudly on the nightstand. When she looked, she realized she'd eaten half her dinner but hadn't spoken a word to him.

"You okay?"

"Tired," she said. "Sorry. And you were so sweet with the bath and the food. I know I'm terrible company."

"Tired? Is that all? Because you sure seem like something else is on your mind."

"No, there's more. It's about Erin. She's not going to get the job she was promised on the sequel."

"Why not?" He looked stunned. "Everyone says she's the backbone of the film."

Lila grinned. "Listen to you sounding like an insider. But you're right. That's what makes everything so awful. Baxter will be named first AD."

"What the hell? The guy has no idea what he's doing."

"I know. It's all about money. Baxter's uncle's check was big enough to ensure his nephew could have the job. And Erin was the cost."

"Even I know that without Erin, the film's going to fall apart. He's an idiot."

"Which is why Erin's agreed to stay. She says she'll be paid as if she's the first AD, and that will help her get out from behind the loan she'd taken out to invest in the movie. Actually she means for it to help us both pay off the loans. She'll also be calling the shots. Baxter won't override her—he just gets all the credit."

Frowning thoughtfully, Clint finished his beer. "What about you? Is your role affected?"

"Nope. I'll still be in it, but it won't be the same."

"I'm sorry," Clint said, rubbing her arm. "I know how much you wanted this to work out."

"Honestly? I'm not even sure I care. Sometimes I think I'd rather just keep doing hair, which is something I enjoy."

"Do you really mean that?"

She sighed. "This business can be brutal. Erin's going to have to put up with Baxter's incompetence, and knowing every day that Jason sold her out. I don't even know how she's going to do it. She can barely tolerate Baxter or Jason now." Lila began collecting the takeout boxes. "But Erin doesn't give up easily. She can take a lot, always the optimist, waiting for that right door to open."

Clint was finished, too, so she stuffed all the containers back into the empty bags, and set them next to the wastebasket by the dresser.

By the time she was back in bed, she felt as if taking one more step might just kill her. Not that she wanted to disappoint Clint, but she wasn't sure she had it in her to do much more than kiss him good-night.

He smiled at her. "How about we go brush our teeth, then you crawl into my arms and try to get some sleep?"

"You're joking, right?"

"I can see you're beat. If you want to talk, I'll listen until morning, but I'm hoping you'll conk out. You need the rest."

She leaned over and kissed him, and while she meant for it to be a quick peck, she found she wanted it to be more. He tasted like salt and beer, and he smelled wonderful. She wasn't even sure why he was being so nice when she was so preoccupied, but she was grateful.

CLINT WAS TEMPTED to touch her, take the kiss and spin it into what he'd been thinking about for the last thirty-six hours, but she really did sound whipped.

So he pulled back. "Let's go brush our teeth."

She nodded and gave him a soft smile. It seemed like she needed a friendly ear, and that's what she'd get.

Even as he stood next to her in the small bathroom, trying hard not to stare at her breasts in the mirror, it occurred to him that if this thing with Erin blew up and she walked, Lila could leave, too. Go back to California tomorrow. Or the next day.

For a minute he'd gotten excited when she'd claimed she didn't care about the part anymore. But he knew it was just exhaustion and disappointment talking. And even if she'd meant it, that wasn't the same as saying she was done with Hollywood, just this film and Jason.

She would of course go right back home, get her agent or whatever to send her out on auditions. And she'd get roles, too. Plenty of them. Probably do better once she wasn't tied to all the crap going on with Jason and Baxter and everything else. Anyway, like she'd said the other night, she wouldn't disappoint Erin or her parents.

He looked at Lila, met her gaze, but only for a split second, before she made her way back to the bed. She wasn't eager to talk about it, which he understood. She was hurting and probably hadn't meant half of what she'd said. He only hoped she wouldn't be too embarrassed to use him as a sounding board.

Although, what did he know about her situation? He wasn't even in the business. He might be the nice guy who poured her a bath and bought her dinner, but he wasn't her long-haul guy. Never had been, not for Lila. But that was the deal, wasn't it?

He wiped his mouth, then turned off the bathroom light. As for him, it was too late. Foolish, pitiful hick that he was, he'd already fallen for her. Hard.

18

AFTER A SURPRISINGLY good night's sleep, Lila was feeling sort of decent at her 6:00 a.m. call. Her actors hadn't arrived yet, and she regretted not taking time to have coffee with Clint before he'd dropped her off. Annoyed, she refused to drink the craft services coffee when she knew there was really great Colombian in the production trailer. If she interrupted a meeting, so what. Everyone would just get over it.

Walking to the trailer, the only nice one of the bunch, she hurried, more because of the cold than anything, and darted up the three stairs. There was no one inside, but someone had been, and the pot of dark roast was waiting for her as if she'd made an appointment.

She'd just grabbed a mug when the door in the back closed with a bang. Turning her head, she saw it was Jason, and her desire for coffee diminished. Not that she wasn't going to take some; she just couldn't look at him without feeling a little sick.

"Hey, you stealing the coffee again?"

"As if I haven't earned a decent cup," she said. She poured, careful not to let her tremble make her spill the coffee, and by the time she put in a dash of real cream, she couldn't stand it anymore.

She turned to face Jason, who was staring up at the monitor plugged in above the desk.

"Why, Jason?"

He clicked off the dailies with the remote and blinked at her. "Why what?"

"Why was it so easy to sell out Erin? After all she's done for you? After we all swore we'd never become *that*."

"Oh, please. Look, I know you and Erin are besties, and you think I've screwed her, but has she told you that I'm paying her full salary for a first AD? It's not all that terrible."

"Of course it is. Good grief, how you've rationalized everything you used to believe was wrong about the business. Erin is the only thing that truly kept this shoot going. Making Baxter AD is a slap in her face, and you know it."

She could see the red rising up Jason's neck, a sure sign he was ready to blow. Well, she didn't care. Not a whit.

"What, you think it was an easy call for me? Do you have any idea how much money we've got now? Enough to make our budget on the sequel. Without taking out any more loans. Paul Mortimer's check isn't all I've got. He has connections to distributors. My God, after all these years, are you truly this naive?"

"I know who you were. And who you are now. And you used to believe the film would speak for itself. Despite everything, it's a hell of a movie, Jason. You didn't need to sell out. You just got scared and sold your soul for the easier road."

"Christ, what, has Erin been giving you lessons on breaking my balls?"

"I don't need lessons to tell the truth."

"What are you so upset about, anyway? You've still got your part. You're going to get some action on that role, sweetheart. That's what you've always wanted, and I just made sure it would happen. You should be thanking me. I'm giving you a future that's not working in a crappy trailer on some other actress's hair."

For a moment, Lila couldn't catch her breath. Then she got really, really calm. She put her mug down and took a step forward, then another, until she was right up in Jason's face. "You know what? I quit. I'm done. I don't want to work with you ever again. And I sure as heck don't want Baxter telling me what to do for a good eight weeks. I'll finish up on this one, because I've signed a contract, but after that? No more, Jason. Not one extra day."

"You're joking."

"Do I look like I'm joking?"

"This is your shot, Lila. For God's sake, you've got talent. We wrote this character for you. Tara's gonna get as much print as the lead. Don't you understand? This is the part that has all the juice. Don't walk away when it finally matters. You'll be back at square one, can't you see that?"

"I see everything quite clearly, thank you. You're thirty years old and you look like you're forty, you know that? Your affair with Penelope is doing damage to the movie, and your reputation. You sold out your most loyal friend and told her about it after the fact. I'm absolutely certain you knew she'd stick around, because that's who Erin is. Honorable. And you stuck a knife in her back. You—" Her brain and mouth both seemed to quit on her. "You stupid fucker. I'd rather wait tables than work with you again."

Lila's heart was beating so hard she might just have a stroke. She'd never felt better or been surer about anything in her life. And she'd used the F-word. She walked out of the trailer with her head held high.

Until she realized she'd just quit without talking to Erin.

How could she have been so stupid? It wasn't as if she could go back and say, by the way, please don't tell Erin. Pretty, pretty please. For old times' sake. And p.s. you're still a stupid fucker.

Lila sighed.

Crap.

CLINT DIDN'T KNOW what was going on when he saw Lila leave the trailer looking so angry she could spit, but when he saw Jason running after her, Clint jumped out of his truck.

Jason was calling out to her, and she just kept shaking her head, moving fast, without looking back at him. She was at work, Jason was still her boss, and since she didn't appear to be in any danger, Clint had no right to interfere. But that was just too damn bad. She could chew him out later if she wanted.

She was still a good distance away, and he doubted she'd seen him yet. Her head was bowed as she stared at the ground in front of her.

Jason gave up his pursuit, whether it was because he'd seen Clint, he didn't know. Didn't care. As he closed in on Lila, he saw how pale she looked. The violence building inside him wasn't anything he'd ever experienced before, and his fists reflexively clenched.

God help Jason if he was responsible for the stricken expression on her face.

Clint stopped ten feet in front of her.

"Lila?" he said, realizing she hadn't noticed him. "Sweetheart?"

Startled, she glanced up and froze. "Hi. What are you doing here?"

He held up her cell phone. "You forgot this in the truck."

"Oh." She patted her pocket, then held out her hand. "Thanks, I would've been lost without it."

"What's wrong?"

"Nothing." Her shoulders slumped. "Is Jason behind me?"

"He went back to his trailer."

"Good." She drew in a deep breath. "Look, I can't talk. I've got to get to work."

He followed her gaze to the man and woman, actors with small parts, who were here for the week.

Lila touched his arm with an unsteady hand. "Everything's fine," she said. "I promise I'll call you later." She looked as if she was in some kind of daze. "I just quit."

"You what?"

"I quit," she repeated. "You can't say anything."

She smiled at the approaching couple and said, "Go to the trailer, I'll be right there." She looked back at Clint. "Don't tell anyone, okay?"

He was almost too shocked to speak. "I won't."

"It's fine," she said, her face a complete wreck. "I promise."

He might've believed her if her voice hadn't cracked. Twice. Both times when she'd said the word *quit*. Given her loyalty to Erin, he could see her telling Jason to shove it on her friend's behalf. But things sure weren't fine. He recognized regret when he heard it.

Watching her race up the trailer steps, he couldn't make himself move. He had an order to pick up at the hardware store. He'd figured on hanging around and having breakfast at the diner while he waited for Jorgenson to open. But the thought of food didn't agree with him now.

Cast, crew and extras were arriving in herds. He'd left his truck in a lousy spot. He had to move it before he jammed someone up. Part of him wanted to wait around, be available if Lila had a few minutes to talk. But what was the point? Of course he wanted to make sure she was okay, that was a given. It was that tiny niggling of hope that worried him. The hope he still harbored that if she really had quit and it stuck, that could mean something for their future together.

On the other hand, if things went further south with Jason, she could be gone by the end of the day. She wanted to be at home for Christmas. If Jason refused to give her back the role, this was a great opportunity for her to tell him to stick it.

He climbed into his truck and sat there taking one deep breath after another. Just to slow his heart rate. Hell, at least he had the sense to be concerned. Because he knew her quitting didn't change anything. He'd figured that out last night.

Lila had expected to be busy today. But damn, he hoped she took a moment to call him. He sat there for another five minutes, staring at his phone, fighting the impulse to call her. But he was blocking traffic. If he didn't move, someone would be coming to chase him off the lot.

He drove to town, parked in front of the diner and

laid his head back. Lila had slept well, but he hadn't. He needed more coffee, and in a minute he'd rally and go get some.

What he had to remember, Lila may have doubts and regrets over quitting, but he didn't have any doubts about his future. He couldn't afford to, because he belonged at the Whispering Pines, keeping the Landers' name and tradition alive. Clint hoped Lila was right about Seth wanting to come back to the family. But they couldn't count on him.

Anyway, that wasn't the point. Tomorrow made three weeks. That's how long he'd known Lila. And he'd been driving himself insane about *their future*? That pretty much said it all. He was the worst kind of fool.

Clint hadn't realized he'd closed his eyes until someone knocked on the window. He straightened with a start. What the hell?

He let down the window. "Mom? What are you doing here? It's early."

She smiled. "Early? It's eight forty. How about buying your old mom a cup of coffee?"

Clint stared at the dashboard clock. An hour had gone by. How was that possible?

"Looks as though you could use some yourself."

Dazed, he glanced at her. "Sure," he said, and climbed out.

They sat in a small booth at the back of the diner and ordered coffee right away. "I'm so glad I caught you alone," his mom said and reached across the table to pat his hand.

"Is that why you're in town?"

"No," she said, laughing. "I need to pick up a few things at Abe's Variety. Although I wouldn't mind spotting a movie star or two."

Clint smiled. "I don't think any of them are in town today."

"Is Lila working?"

He nodded, hoping the conversation wasn't about to get awkward. "What is it you wanted to talk about?"

"You taking over the ranch."

Clint nodded at the waitress as she set down their coffees, and then he looked at his mom. "Didn't Dad tell you I gave him my answer?"

"He did." She stirred sugar into her cup. "And I'm so proud of him for telling you to wait."

Clint sighed. He knew she meant well, but damn... "It'll be the same answer after Christmas."

"Have you said anything to Lila?"

"She has nothing to do with it, Mom."

"Don't you think she should?"

He turned to stare out the window for a minute. "Look, do I like her? Very much. Can I see the two of us together in a year? No. She's an actress. She plays it down, but in a few months she'll have a part in a movie that will be a major game changer for her—"

"Oh, for goodness' sake, I know all about that," she said, waving a hand. "And about that Caribbean cruise your dad booked, too. So don't let that influence your decision."

"How?"

Laughing, she shook her head. "Your dad, bless his heart, forgets I pay the bills. I saw the charge on last month's statement. In fact, I've got to pick up some Scotch tape to leave around before he drives me crazy looking for it. I'm assuming he wants to wrap the tickets."

"And Lila?"

"We had a few private minutes in the kitchen."

"What did she say?" Clint put down his cup.

"First, the woman clearly has feelings for you, Clint, and don't act like I don't know what I'm talking about. Because you have feelings for her, too—pretty strong feelings that might be making your thinking fuzzy."

"Mom," he said calmly, "what did Lila say?"

"It's more what she didn't say."

His heart sunk. He should've known...

"That girl isn't cut out for show business. You say she plays it down, the big part that's coming up? Lila isn't playing it down, Clinton. She doesn't have the heart for it."

He swallowed. This was torture. He wanted to believe that, even while he told himself his mom was wrong.

"You listen when she talks about being in the movies. It *used* to be her dream. It isn't anymore."

He stared at his cup. Sure, he'd thought the same thing. For a minute. Before he'd realized he was being a fool. "And what if you're wrong?"

"Well, if I am, it doesn't change the fact that Lila isn't Anne."

He met his mom's concerned gaze.

"I know it crossed your mind, and then some," she said. "I'd be worried if it hadn't. Lila is different. She's had a taste of what it's like to be in all the Hollywood hoopla, and it's not for her. She's more of a homebody. Glamour and fame will never take the place of having family around her. And yes, I know you're gonna say I met her for just one night, what do I know, but here's something else to consider. Her looks can be deceiving. Might be hard to imagine her chasing after snotty-nosed kids and muddy dogs."

Clint smiled a little at that. The thing was, he could

see it. Her. Him. The two of them chasing after kids in the damn house he wanted to build. That was the problem. Lila was loyal to Erin, and she didn't want to disappoint her parents. He admired that, but it was another stumbling block. It also lent credence to what his mom said about her losing interest in the dream.

But he'd seen the regret in her face. He'd heard it in her voice. He wouldn't be surprised if she was talking to Jason right now. Apologizing. Trying to get the role back. And if she didn't, she'd always wonder how her life and career could've turned out differently.

That would kill him the most. Watching her spend the rest of her life regretting that she hadn't made it to the finish line. And always wondering what might've happened if she'd just gotten that big break she'd worked so hard to get.

He thought about Nathan and the hell his brother had gone through after Anne died. Not knowing about the yearning his wife had kept secret had almost destroyed him. Clint agreed. Lila wasn't anything like Anne, but to wonder was human nature.

"Clint, do your old mom a favor." She waited until he looked at her. "Before you give up, talk to Lila. Ask her what she wants."

Lila had battled against nervous energy all day. That, and guilt. She had to talk to Erin, who was crazy busy. Everyone was, including Jason, so just maybe he hadn't said anything to Erin.

At 5:00 o'clock she texted Erin their SOS signal. It meant drop everything, screw everyone, come now.

As she waited, Lila bit her nails. She'd quit the nasty habit eight years ago. Another reason to hate Jason the

Weasel. "What?" Erin came running up behind her. "Are you okay?"

"Yes. Maybe." Lila swallowed hard. "I love you. You're not like a sister to me, you are my sister. You know that, right?"

"Lila, you're scaring the shit out of me. So just say it."

They were standing between two trailers. People could see them, but not hear the conversation. It was the best location Lila could manage.

"First, promise you won't hate me." Lila wouldn't cry. She'd promised herself.

"You could never do anything to make me hate you," Erin said. "Oh, unless you don't start talking."

Lila gave her a shaky smile. "I quit. This morning."

"You did not."

Lila nodded. "I know I should've talked to you first, but Jason made me so angry I just—"

"Don't worry, kiddo." Erin rubbed Lila's arm. "He hasn't given the role away. I'll talk to him."

"Erin, no. What I'm trying to say is—" She needed to breathe. "I don't want it. I can't do this anymore. I feel terrible. I do. We made promises…we had plans…" Lila sniffed. "Oh, and I called him a stupid fucker."

Erin blinked. "You?"

Lila nodded.

"To his face?"

Lila sighed.

Erin let out a howl and hugged her. "I'm so proud! Pissed that I wasn't there to see it, but really proud."

She freed herself from Erin's strong grasp. "You understand what I'm saying, don't you? It's not just Jason. I don't want this anymore, Erin. I hate being on location. I hate the—"

Erin's and Lila's phones buzzed within seconds of each other. It was the second time for Erin, so she brought out her cell.

Lila read hers. Clint wanted to see her tonight. She felt so giddy with relief, she texted him to come anytime.

"I have five minutes tops," Erin said. "But I have a confession, too."

CLINT'S PALMS WERE SWEATING, so was the back of his neck. He used a towel he had on the backseat, then got out of the truck. Lila's text had said to meet her at the hair-and-makeup trailer. He saw her coming from the back of the lot, but Baxter intercepted her.

For once he didn't want to strangle the guy. Clint slowed his pace and used the extra time to steady his breathing. He was going to do just as his mom suggested. Ask Lila. Straight out. She might give him a pitying look, but she wouldn't laugh at him.

Lila was giving Baxter the strangest look, so Clint sped up.

His back was to Clint. "You know, if you'd just be a little nicer to me, I can make things happen for you," Baxter said, reaching a hand out to Lila, who started laughing.

"You bastard," Clint said, and yanked the guy around to face him. His fist slammed into Baxter's jaw, and the man stumbled back.

"Clint!" Lila grabbed his arm and stopped him from taking another swing. "He's not worth it."

Baxter sputtered, red-faced, trying to breathe. Several bystanders applauded.

"Please," Lila said, trying to drag him away. "I already quit. Who cares what the slimeball says?"

Clint looked at her. Something was different about her voice. She didn't sound upset like she had earlier. She led him to the trailer, but they didn't go inside. "Are you saying you can't get the role back? Is Jason being hard-nosed?"

"Why would I want it back?" She seemed genuinely puzzled.

"You're not having second thoughts? Because you sure looked like it this morning."

"I was upset because I hadn't told Erin first. I haven't felt this good in forever." She laughed, and the happy sound clutched at his heart. "I'm finished. With all of it."

Clint took her hand. "You've worked a long time for this. I hate to see you have any regrets or wonder what could've been…"

"You're right. I've been at this for a very long time. That's how I can be so sure it's not what I want. This didn't happen overnight, Clint. Being on location and away from my family, and seeing the double-dealing up close… I'm not cut out for this."

"What about Erin?"

Tears glistened in Lila's eyes, and Clint felt his little bit of hope disappear. "Erin's quitting, too. She was staying on to make sure Jason let me have the role."

"She's quitting the business?"

"Not completely. She's got a fantastic idea for another documentary. She won an award for her last one."

The new information was making Clint's head spin. He wasn't sure what to say.

"I thought you'd be happy for me," Lila said softly.

He met her steady gaze. "I want you to be sure, sweetheart, that's all."

"Look, you're going to believe what you want, but

I'm telling you, I'm done. And I'm walking away for me." She turned her hand over and entwined their fingers. "Hollywood was a fun dream—the best," she said. "For a kid with stars in her eyes. I'm twenty-eight. I want to get married, have children, and I want to be there for them, always, just like my mom was there for me and my brother and sister. I know it's not chic or popular to admit, but that's what I want."

Clint could barely breathe let alone swallow. Neither of them had looked away once. He thought he could read her. But was he wishing for too much? "What do you plan on doing after you finish here?"

"Well, I miss my family like crazy," she said, and his heart sank. Lila wouldn't leave California. "So I'll go visit them for a couple weeks. When Erin moves ahead with the documentary, I figure I'll help with that."

They had ranches in California, quite a few from what he'd heard. Maybe it was time to have a talk with Seth. "What about after that?"

"I'm not sure." Lila looked nervous. Damn, he'd started sweating five minutes ago. "Have anything in mind?" She put a tentative hand on his chest, her beautiful blue eyes brimming with hope.

Relief and joy flowed through him like a spring river. Clint put his arms around her. "Actually I'm going to talk to a guy about building a house. Wouldn't mind some input if you're willing."

"Yes," she said, smiling through tears and hugging his neck. "Yes."

Clint froze. He did a quick replay in his head. Marriage had been on his mind for a few days. Had he just asked her to— No, he was pretty sure he hadn't done that.

He leaned back and looked at her. "Lila, I love you."

She nodded and whispered, "I love you."

"You know we've only known each other three weeks."

"I keep reminding myself of that," she said. "It seems like so much longer."

"And I think you know I have responsibilities here."

"I do know that," she whispered, snuggling up closer. "But I hope you can take a few days off to come with me and meet my parents."

Clint's chest tightened. He managed to nod. "Lila, will you marry me?"

"Yes," she replied, laughing and kissing him hard.

He held her close, breathing in her familiar scent, long after the applause around them stopped.

* * * * *

REQUEST YOUR FREE BOOKS!
2 FREE NOVELS PLUS 2 FREE GIFTS!

⊕ HARLEQUIN®

Blaze®

red-hot reads!

SPECIAL EXCERPT FROM

⬦HARLEQUIN®

Blaze

*Veronica "Flash" Redding hates that she's in love
with her boss, Ian Asher, but that doesn't stop her from
seducing him. And together, in the bedroom, they are
creating the hottest December on record!*

*Read on for a sneak preview of
ONE HOT DECEMBER,
book three of Tiffany Reisz's sexy holiday trilogy
MEN AT WORK.*

"You dumped me after one night and said you couldn't
date an inferior."

"I didn't say that. I said I was your superior and
therefore could not date you. You remember that part
about me being your boss?"

"Only for two more weeks."

"What are you going to do?"

"I got a new job. A better job."

"Better? Better than here?"

She almost rolled her eyes.

"Yes, Ian, believe it or not. I would also like to have
a job where I don't weld all day and then go home and
weld some more for my other life. You can't blame me
for that."

"I don't, no. You've stuck it out here longer than
anyone thought you would."

"I had to fight tooth and nail to earn the respect of
the crew. I'm a little tired of fighting to be treated like a
human being. You can't blame me for that, either."

So, yeah, she was thrilled about the new job.

But.

But…Ian.

It wasn't just that he was good in bed. He was. She remembered all too well that he was—passionate, intense, sensual, powerful, dominating, everything she wanted in a man. The first kiss had been electric. The second intoxicating. By the third she would have sold her soul to have him inside her before morning, but he didn't ask for her soul, only every inch of her body, which she'd given him for hours. When she'd gone to bed with him that night, she'd been half in love with him. By the time she left it the next morning, she was all the way in.

Then he'd dumped her.

Six months ago. She ought to be over it by now. She wanted to be over it the day it happened but her heart wasn't nearly as tough as her reputation. The worst part of it all? Ian had been right to dump her. They'd both lost their heads after a couple drinks had loosened their tongues enough to admit they were attracted to each other. But Ian had a company to run and there were rules—good ones—that prohibited the man who signed the paychecks from sleeping with the woman who wielded the torch.

Don't miss ONE HOT DECEMBER
by Tiffany Reisz, available December 2016 everywhere
Harlequin® Blaze® books and ebooks are sold.

www.Harlequin.com

Reading Has Its Rewards

Earn **FREE BOOKS!**

Register at **Harlequin My Rewards** and submit your Harlequin purchases from wherever you shop to earn points for free books and other exclusive rewards.

Plus submit your purchases from now till May 30th for a chance to win a $500 Visa Card*.

Visit **HarlequinMyRewards.com** today

Earn **FREE** REWARDS HarlequinMyRewards.com Join Today!

MYR16R1

AT THE BRINK

by

ANNA DEL MAR

What begins as a contractual arrangement turns into a tale of intrigue, dark lust and sexual obsessions.

He's a decorated war hero and former SEAL.

She's trapped in a dangerous situation.

And he's made her an offer she can't refuse.

"This author has captured my attention with her well-written words, strong characters, and vivid storyline."
—*Harlequin Junkie*

Get your copy now!

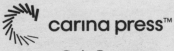

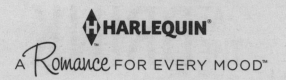